PUFFIN B

Stars

Luke Jennings is the author of three novels, including the Booker Prize-nominated *Atlantic*. His memoir, *Blood Knots*, was shortlisted for the Samuel Johnson and William Hill prizes. Before becoming a writer, Luke trained as a dancer and worked with classical and contemporary companies for ten years. He is currently the dance critic at the *Observer*, and has also written for *Vanity Fair* and the *New Yorker.*

You're less likely to know his daughter, Laura Jennings, who is twelve and lives with her parents, two brothers and her dog Dusty. She says, 'At school I'm quite sporty but I like drama best, because I have always enjoyed acting, singing and performing. I love books, and my favourite author is Stephen King.'

LAURA & LUKE JENNINGS

PUFFIN

PUFFIN BOOKS

Published by the Penguin Group
Penguin Books Ltd, 80 Strand, London WC2R ORL, England
Penguin Group (USA) Inc., 375 Hudson Street, New York, New York 10014, USA
Penguin Group (Canada), 90 Eglinton Avenue East, Suite 700, Toronto, Ontario, Canada M4P 2Y3
(a division of Pearson Penguin Canada Inc.)
Penguin Ireland, 25 St Stephen's Green, Dublin 2, Ireland
(a division of Penguin Books Ltd)
Penguin Group (Australia), 707 Collins Street, Melbourne, Victoria 3008, Australia
(a division of Pearson Australia Group Pty Ltd)
Penguin Books India Pvt Ltd, 11 Community Centre, Panchsheel Park, New Delhi – 110 017, India
Penguin Group (NZ), 67 Apollo Drive, Rosedale, Auckland 0632, New Zealand
(a division of Pearson New Zealand Ltd)
Penguin Books (South Africa) (Pty) Ltd, Block D, Rosebank Office Park, 181 Jan Smuts Avenue,
Parktown North, Gauteng 2193, South Africa

Penguin Books Ltd, Registered Offices: 80 Strand, London WC2R ORL, England

puffinbooks.com

First published 2013

001

Typeset in 13.5/16pt Baskerville by Palimpsest Book Production Ltd, Falkirk, Stirlingshire

Printed in Great Britain by Clays Ltd, St Ives plc

British Library Cataloguing in Publication Data

A CIP catalogue record for this book is available from the British Library

ISBN: 978-0-141-34440-9

www.greenpenguin.co.uk

For Nicky (aka Mum)

I

'Well,' said Peter Bailey. 'Here we are!'

Jess looked about her. To her left, blue and gold against the roadside trees, was a large painted sign.

In front of her was pair of iron gates, and beyond these, half hidden by trees, was a large red-brick building. She felt a sinking feeling and a sudden, sharp loneliness. She had wanted this so much, but now that the moment had come . . .

Her father switched off the car engine, and reached for her hand. 'You'll be fine,' he smiled, squeezing her fingers.

'And what about you, Dad? Will you be fine, without me to look after you?'

'I promise.'

They drove through the gates and up the gravel driveway. To Jess's relief, no bits fell off their ancient car as they did so. That would have been just *too* embarrassing. Close up, the school looked huge, old and a little shabby. Other cars were parked in front of the entrance, and half a dozen boys and girls – mostly around fourteen, Jess guessed – were standing around chatting. As she got out of the car they glanced at her, and one of the boys walked over. He was wearing a faded Radiohead T-shirt and had dark, untidy hair. A gold stud shone in his left ear.

'You look, like, *new*,' he said with a grin.

'Er . . . yeah,' said Jess, struck by his confidence. But then this was a stage school, so perhaps it wasn't so surprising.

Suddenly she felt self-conscious. She hadn't known what to wear for the first day so had put on the red school tracksuit. Wrong! Everyone else was wearing their own stuff. As she watched, a slim, sharp-featured girl walked past in shredded combats. The sides of her head were shaved and her hair gelled into little punky points. *Bat-girl*, thought Jess.

'That's Spike,' said the boy. 'She's pretty nutty, even for this place . . . But how come you're joining now, in the summer term? All the other first years have been here since September.'

'I know. Long story. I've got a lot of catching up to do.'

'You'll be fine.'

'I hope so.' His eyes, she noticed, were a clear, icy blue.

As soon as she'd spoken, her father appeared beside her with her suitcase.

The boy stared at them. 'The girls' dorm block's at the back of the main building,' he said, pointing. 'You should register with the office and then get your stuff over there.'

'OK,' said Jess. 'Thanks!'

He raised a hand, smiled, and turned away. He looked completely at home. Exactly the opposite of how Jess felt, right then.

'I guess we should go and register,' said her dad, lifting her suitcase.

'Guess we should.'

Jess had met the school principal, Miss Allen, at the audition. She was elegant, silver-haired, and a little scary, but smiled as she welcomed Jess to the school. There was some paperwork to sign with Mr Dye, the school secretary, and then they were back outside again, and it was time to say goodbye.

'I mean it, Dad. I'll be fine. Please. Just . . . leave the suitcase and go.'

'OK, Jess.' He gave her a quick, tight hug. 'I'll see you . . .'

'Soon, yeah?'

'I promise.' He bent down and kissed the top of her head. She closed her eyes, and when she opened them again he was gone.

2

Minutes later Jess was standing, suitcase in hand, in an echoing first-floor corridor that smelt faintly of floor polish. Other girls hurried past her, dragging suitcases and calling out to each other. Some of them slowed for a moment to glance at Jess in her red tracksuit. There was the distant sound of running feet and slamming doors.

A notice board above a radiator held lists of names and room numbers.

Upper Gallery Room 10, she read. *Eleanor Fox, Ashanti Taylor, Verity Nash, Jessica Bailey.*

This was it then. Until that moment it had not really sunk in that she was going to a boarding school. That she would be sleeping here, night after night, week after week, month after . . . Never in her life had she so longed for her room at home. It was small, and it was usually pretty untidy, but it was hers, full of the things she'd grown up with. And now, for what seemed like *forever*, she had to share a room with strangers. Taking a deep breath, she pushed the door open.

The room had four narrow iron beds in it, and hadn't seen a new coat of paint in years. On the wall next to the window was a small mirror, on which someone had written 'Fame and Fortune' in marker pen. One of the beds was taken, with a suitcase beneath it and a bright red dressing gown and pink nightdress draped across it. A glance at the label on the case told her that it belonged to Ashanti Taylor.

Jess was just wondering which of the other beds to choose – there were two beneath the windows and one behind the door – when a willowy figure swept into the room. It was the bat-girl. Earphone wires trailed from her head to her hip pocket and she was carrying a bulky backpack.

'Hi,' said Jess.

The girl didn't answer, just gave her a wave and slung her pack on to the bed behind the door. Then, turning, she pointed to the bed nearest it and smiled questioningly.

'Er, yeah. Sure,' said Jess, a little irritated that the girl couldn't even be bothered to speak to her. Swinging her case on to the bed, Jess started to unpack into the nearest chest of drawers. Her dance gear took up the most space. Ballet shoes, jazz shoes, leg warmers, leotards and the rest of it. Apart from this, and the regulation school clothing, she didn't have much. Her laptop and her phone. Jeans, trainers, a couple of hoodies, a few T-shirts, some underwear, and that was about it.

Spike – wasn't that what the boy had said her name was? – was another story. Unzipping her backpack, she poured the contents on to the bed – a rainbow cascade of belts, tights, scarves, wristbands, scrunchies, fingerless gloves, bandanas, make-up boxes, hair-gel, perfume sprays and nail polish. Jess was staring enviously at it all when the door swung open.

'Yay, Spike! And you must be Jessica Bailey?' The speaker was a girl of mixed race, amber eyes in a heart-shaped face, hair cut in a short, fashionable bob.

Jess nodded, returning the girl's smile. 'And you're . . . Ashanti, right?'

'I'm Ash, yeah. And you've met Spike? Her real name's Verity, if you're wondering, but no one actually calls her that.'

'Er, well, we've . . .'

'She's deaf,' said Ash breezily, swinging the door shut behind her. 'You've probably gathered that.'

Jess glanced at the other girl, eyes widening, not quite sure what to say, and Spike shrugged back, as if telling her: *Don't worry about it – it's no big deal.*

'She lip-reads brilliantly,' said Ash. 'So you can talk to her all you want.'

Spike bowed, grinning broadly, and Jess smiled back. She'd never met a deaf person before. And this was a stage school, which seemed just about the most unlikely place in the world to find someone who . . . well, who couldn't hear.

'She's a dancer,' said Ash, as if reading her thoughts. 'She was born partially deaf, but the amazing thing is that she can hear music.'

Spike's fingers fluttered briefly.

'She says it's the vibrations,' Ash said. 'She sort of half feels them, half hears them.'

'So was that sign language?' asked Jess.

'Yup. We've all learnt a bit.'

'Wow! Is it difficult?'

'It is, quite. But there are lots of good websites where you can learn. And it's fun too. Like a secret language.'

Jess nodded. Learning sign language did sound sort of fun and, if she was to be friends with Spike, she'd have to give it a try. Right now, though, it just felt like one more challenge she would have to face.

Jess had done singing and dancing classes since she was at primary school. To start with she'd been pushed by her mother, who'd always dreamt of a career on the stage. It had also helped that the church hall where the classes took place was just one stop on the bus from her school, so she'd gone there every day.

Gradually, she'd come to love it. The daily ritual of the classes, the familiar sound of the old upright piano, the tutus and tote bags, the suede-soled jazz and ballet shoes from Freed of London. She even enjoyed the exams. For the ballet grades their teacher, Miss Julie, would put the girls' hair up in buns and braid them with miniature silk roses. For her musical theatre grades Jess and her mum would improvise costumes and props. A swimsuit for songs from *South Pacific*, a cowboy hat for *Oklahoma*, a flowery skirt for *Showboat*.

Best of all were the end-of-term shows. Somewhere, at the bottom of a drawer at home, Jess still had the pink satin rabbit-ears she'd worn aged six. Right from the start, she had loved performing. It wasn't so much the challenge of the singing and the dancing; it was the sheer excitement of being on stage. That magical feeling of being an ordinary person one minute, and then, with the help of a costume and a dab of make-up, turning into someone completely different.

'You've got a real talent, Jess,' Miss Julie had

told her. And it was true. In that little world, she'd shone.

Whether she would shine at Arcadia was another matter altogether. Here, she knew, everyone had been the best in their class and in their school. The best singers, the best dancers, the best actors. If Jess was going to survive – and she was determined that she *would* survive – she'd have to push herself harder than she had in her life.

'Did you share a room last year?' she asked Ash.

'Yeah. The Fatal Four. Me, Spike, Foxy and Eve. Eve left. That's her bed you're taking.'

'Wow,' Jess stared at her. 'I mean, I'm sorry. That's . . .'

'It's fine,' said Ash, swinging her suitcase on to her bed and popping the catch. 'Don't worry about it.'

Jess frowned. When people told you not to worry, that was the time to start worrying. The four of them had obviously been really good friends. Why had Eve left?

Her musings were interrupted by a brisk knock at the door. 'Good afternoon, girls. Ashanti, Verity . . . and you must be Jessica.'

The speaker was a neatly dressed woman in her forties with a sharp, bird-like gaze. Jess nodded, a little nervously.

'Excellent. Welcome to Arcadia. I'm Miss Pearl. You're something of a dancer, I gather?'

'Er . . . a bit.'

'Well, I expect we'll soon find out.' She looked briskly round the room. 'Eleanor's not yet back, I see?'

'Not yet,' said Ash, glancing at Spike.

'Hmm. I hope she's not going to be late again, or –' At that moment Miss Pearl's phone trilled. She left the room.

'Wow!' breathed Jess. 'She's scary.'

Ash nodded. 'She's head of ballet. And you're right, she's dead scary, specially if you've got two left feet, like me. Spike, of course, gets away with murder . . .'

Spike grinned, and curtseyed. Then, a questioning look in her eye, lifted her arms and circled her hands around each other above her head.

'She says, are you really a dancer?' Ash translated.

Jess shrugged. 'Well, I've done ballet classes since forever,' she began. 'But I wouldn't say I was that brilliant.'

'So what was La Perla going on about?'

'I think she meant my audition,' replied Jess, wincing. 'God, I go hot and cold all over just thinking about it.'

'Tell,' said Ash firmly, and Spike nodded.

Jess took a deep breath. The audition had taken place three months earlier. Most of the other boys and girls there had been thirteen-year-olds, auditioning to join the first year the following September. But there had been a dozen girls – Jess one of them – who were hoping to start the following term, in the summer.

'There was just one place,' said Ash. 'The school knew by then that Eve was leaving.'

'*One place!*' yelped Jess. 'Thank God I didn't know that then. I'd have completely lost it. As it was I had this whole kind of freeze-up, freak-out-type experience.'

'Go on,' commanded Ash, and Spike nodded enthusiastically.

'Well, I'd done the drama and the singing, and there was only the jazz-ballet and the classical left. So I went into this huge studio, with all these people sitting at this long table, and a guy at the piano, and it was just awful, because you know they tell you to prepare a dance? Well, I'd learnt this routine to "Superstar" by Jamelia, but I was suddenly like *a hundred per cent certain* that I'd forgotten every single step of it. Which was totally crazy because I'm really not someone who forgets routines. Like ever. So it must have been some sort of audition thing.'

'Omigod,' said Ash. 'I so know that feeling.'

'Anyway, I totally panicked and asked the guy at the piano to play whatever he liked. So all the people at the table look at each other, like *please*, who *is* this person, and the piano guy shrugs and starts to play this tinkly ballet music from *The Nutcracker* or whatever. At which point all my steps suddenly come back to me, and I start doing my "Superstar" thing and, weirdly, it kind of *fits*. I mean, it wasn't brilliant, but it was different, and by the end I could see they were smiling. So, you know. Kind of worked out. And then there was the actual ballet bit, with pointe work and everything, and by then I was so hyper that I just went for it flat out. And I got through it. So . . . yeah. That's what happened.'

'Wow,' said Ash. 'And here you are!'

'Yes, here I am. But like they told my dad, I'm here on a trial basis. I've got a term to prove myself.'

The acceptance letter had arrived a week after the audition. She could join the school, the letter informed her, at the beginning of the summer term. But she would need to work hard to catch up with the other first years, who had already spent two terms there. And if she couldn't catch up she wouldn't be offered a second-year place in the autumn.

Ash squeezed her arm. 'You'll be fine.'

Jess glanced at the mirror. 'Fame and Fortune! Who wrote that?'

'Eve. To remind herself why she was here, every time she looked into the mirror. Which was quite often!'

'Why did she leave?' asked Jess.

Ash looked at Spike and then back at Jess. 'Basically, because she couldn't handle it here. The whole performance thing. The competition. She just decided it wasn't for her.'

Jess nodded. 'I see.'

'I didn't want to tell you that. But you'll find out soon enough. Basically, it's not enough to be good; everyone at Arcadia is good. You need more. You have to want this life more than anything else in the world.' She brightened. 'The good news is that you're not facing it all alone. You've got us on your side. Spike, Foxy and me.'

'Thanks. That means a lot. But I haven't even met Foxy.'

'Oh, don't worry,' said Ash breezily. 'Roommates stick together here. First law of survival.'

Jess opened her mouth to speak, but no words came, and tears sprang to her eyes. She turned away, not wanting them to see that she was upset. It wasn't saying goodbye to her dad that had set her off, although that was part of it, and it wasn't

Ash's kindness, although that was part of it too. It was that deep inside herself, she was beginning to think the school was right to have its doubts. Perhaps she wasn't talented enough, or attractive enough, or whatever it was that you had to be to make it through this place. Right now, fame and fortune seemed a very long way away.

3

Taking a deep breath, Jess walked into the dining hall. There was a dip in the excited laughter and chatter and everyone stared at her. After her room-mates had left, she'd stayed behind to change into skinny jeans and a T-shirt, but she was still the new girl. The *only* new girl. It was weird, feeling all those eyes on her, knowing that everyone was wondering what made her special enough to come to Arcadia.

Taking a tray, Jess joined the bustling dinner queue. *Smile*, she told herself. She didn't have much appetite and wasn't tempted by the sweaty-looking gammon slices, so settled for the vegetarian option – some sort of green gloop covered by cheese. *Now, if only I can find a friendly face*, she thought, looking out over the busy dining hall.

She saw table after table of strangers. Pretty good-looking strangers, for the most part. Not unfriendly-looking, but not exactly running over and asking her to join them either. And then her gaze met a pair of ice-blue eyes, noted dark hair and a flash of gold at one ear, and her heart turned over. It was the boy in the Radiohead T-shirt. For a moment she stood there, mouth half open, staring. And then someone bumped a tray into her back and she had to move.

She didn't look back at the boy. Apart from anything else, there wasn't any room at his table. But she could feel her heart beating, and a strange kind of breathlessness.

Looking up, searching the back of the hall, she saw a long, waving arm and a punky bracelet. Spike! And there was Ash, next to her. Loading a plastic beaker of water on to her tray, Jess began to wind her way between the tables, trying to ignore the eyes that looked up at her as she passed. *Be cool, Jess*, she told herself. *Head held high, flash-bulbs popping around her, the great star smiles graciously at her fans –*

And then, terrifyingly, the great star's legs were no longer beneath her. What caused the skid Jess never knew, but just before her backside hit the floor she saw an arc of vegetable purée flying through the air. Then came a bump so hard that she gasped. Yikes. That *really* hurt! But the scream – it was more of a screech, really, and so deafeningly high-pitched that it silenced the entire dining hall – wasn't hers. It came from the table above her.

For several long seconds, Jess didn't dare open her eyes. When she did, they met a gaze bright with fury. Jess stared. Even with green gloop splattered across her face, the figure at the table was a vision. *Like a* Vogue *model*, thought Jess, fascinated and petrified at the same time. Around her, frozen with surprise, sat several other scarily glamorous types.

As Jess stared, the vision began to speak. 'You. Clumsy. Fat. Cow,' she said, picking melted cheese from her honey-blonde hair. 'You will apologize, and you will pay for this T-shirt and these jeans to be dry-cleaned. They're designer, in case you hadn't noticed.'

'I . . . I'm r-really sorry,' stammered Jess, climbing painfully to her feet from among the remains of her dinner. 'I slipped.'

'Your problem, girl. Ten quid for the cleaning bill, please.'

Jess looked despairingly from gaze to unsmiling gaze.

'It was an accident, Shannon,' said Ash, suddenly appearing at Jess's side with Spike. 'Anyone could see that.'

'Get lost, Ashanti Taylor. And you –' she glared at Spike – 'I don't want to hear from you either.'

She clapped her hand to her mouth in mock surprise. 'Oh, I forgot! I'm not likely to, am I?'

Spike's eyes narrowed, and Ash held out a warning hand. 'Get over yourself, Shannon Matthews. And stick your tacky, overpriced clothes in the laundry basket like anyone else.'

Shannon stared at her, then turned to Jess. 'If you can't even walk across the dining hall, what do you think's going to happen when you get on stage?'

There was a moment's silence, and one of the modelly sidekicks sniggered.

'I guess I'll worry about that when I get there,' said Jess.

'Good answer,' said Ash, steering her firmly and rapidly away. 'Now let's get you some more dinner.'

'I've sort of lost my appetite,' said Jess. *I suppose I am a bit clumsy*, she thought, *but I've never thought of myself as fat.*

'You're *not fat*,' said Ash. 'Get back in that food queue!'

'Did you just read my mind?' Jess asked her.

'I did. Because I know exactly how Shannon and her gang like to mess with your head.'

On her way back to the queue, Jess flicked a quick glance at the boy with the gold earring. He was looking at her, as she'd guessed he would be.

Catching her eye, he gave her a sympathetic wink, and once again her heart flipped.

A couple of minutes later, she was safely installed at a table with Ash, Spike and a plate of macaroni cheese. 'Thanks for rescuing me,' Jess said, stabbing at the pasta tubes with her fork.

'Our pleasure,' said Ash as Spike removed an imaginary hat and bowed.

'I haven't exactly made a great start, have I?'

'I don't know . . .' Ash grinned. 'You've managed to get the whole school's attention within an hour of arriving here. That's not bad going!'

Jess turned to Spike, who crossed her eyes like a demented goblin, and then, reaching for the empty water jug, started to make her way towards the counter for a refill.

'Does she ever talk?' asked Jess.

'She can, sort of. She did some speech therapy, years ago. But it's difficult if you haven't grown up listening to people's voices. You worry you're sounding weird, especially in a place like this. So she uses sign language instead. Or text messages. She's a super-fast texter.'

'I bet,' said Jess, overcome with sadness at the thought of Spike's silent childhood.

'Look, you mustn't ever, ever let her think you're feeling sorry for her. She's a tough cookie,

Spike. And, trust me, she can make her feelings known in all sorts of ways. As you'll see!'

When Spike came back with the water jug Ash leant back in her chair and ran her fingers through her neat bob. 'I was just telling Jess that she'll have to learn to read sign language.'

Spike smiled and lifted her hands. Her fingers flickered briefly against her palm, a pretend-weary expression touched her eyes, and somehow Jess had no difficulty in understanding her. 'What*ever*!' she translated triumphantly.

'See,' said Ash. 'You speak it already!'

4

Lying in bed, Jess let her thoughts drift. It was a warm night, and through the open window she could hear the breeze in the spreading branches of the cedar tree that stood alongside the dorm block. A faint whisper of air rippled the curtain, bringing with it the night scent of the lawns and flower beds outside. It was the smell of the countryside in summer, so different from the south London tang of diesel fumes, wet pavements and cooking, and for a moment she felt a rush of homesickness, an intense longing for the ordinary, everyday things of home.

Ash and Spike were both asleep – Ash calm as a statue in her neatly made bed, Spike twitching beneath her duvet, one long arm thrown out to the side. It felt very strange to be sharing a room, to hear two other people breathing just beside her. And it would soon be three. What would this Foxy person be like? She sounded scarily glamorous, but then pretty much everybody was scarily glamorous at Arcadia. And probably terrifyingly gifted too. And beautiful, and thin, and . . . *Stop it*, Jess ordered herself. *You're being paranoid and silly. Ballet class tomorrow. Get some sleep.*

But sleep wouldn't come. Just the sighing of the trees and, distantly, the hooting of an owl. The sound made her think of her dad, who was very much a nightbird, being keen on astronomy. Would he be all right without her, alone in that house? Although not exactly alone, because it was a semi, and there were the Ibrahims next door, and most nights you could hear the *whoop-whoop* of their Hindi film music through the dividing wall. But alone in his half of the house. Without Jess to find his car keys, or to know which mantelpiece he'd left his reading glasses on, or which cushion the remote for the DVD player might have slipped behind. Because for such a clever man – such a brilliant man, in fact – Peter Bailey was incredibly disorganized.

Since The Event, it had been just Jess and her dad at number 43, Mafeking Avenue, London SW17. Neither of them was naturally tidy, and the place was a bit – well, more than a bit – messy. Every corner was stacked with books on obscure subjects and the long-outdated scientific equipment that her dad couldn't resist buying on eBay. 'It'll come in handy one day, you'll see,' he'd promise Jess as they took delivery of yet another box of dusty radio valves, or whatever.

Peter Bailey was an astronomer by night, but by day he was a physics tutor, driving from lesson to lesson in a battered Ford Escort. He could have been a full-time teacher, he told Jess, but this wouldn't leave him enough time for his research on Gas Giants. These, apparently, were some kind of planet, although they made Jess think of overweight men with stomach upsets.

And then The Job had come up. The Job was in Saudi Arabia, at a university where, for some reason, they were very interested in Gas Giants. The pay, her dad said, would change their lives, and Jess had briefly seen herself riding through the desert on a camel, wearing a lot of eyeliner and swathed in turquoise silk. She had imagined sand dunes, exotic palaces and plates piled high with pink and green Turkish delight, although part of her knew that Saudi Arabia couldn't really be anything like this. Might well, in fact, be quite a tricky place in some ways, although definitely more exciting than London SW17, with its grey office blocks and its rainswept pavements and endless traffic. Given a choice between the desert and Mitcham Common, she'd go for the desert any day. And then her dad had broken the news to her:

she wasn't coming. She was staying in Britain. Worse – so much worse as to be unimaginable – she was going to boarding school.

Boarding school. The horror of it. All those posh girls talking about their skiing holidays and looking down their horrible posh noses at her . . .

'It'll be a fantastic opportunity, Jess,' Peter Bailey had pleaded. 'The university will be paying. And you can choose which school you go to. They've sent me a list. Look.'

Thanks a bunch, thought Jess. A list of boarding schools. A bit like asking which department of hell you wanted to spend the next million years in. But at the same time she could see that her dad thought it was all a really good idea, and that he desperately wanted that job in Saudi Arabia. Which sort of twisted her heart, because for ages now it had been just the two of them, watching out for each other.

'It won't be forever, Jess. And it'll allow us to do all sorts of things that, as things stand, we just can't afford.'

The money argument, thought Jess miserably. *Always the money argument.* 'Dad, please. Can't we just carry on as we are?'

'Sweetheart, the short answer is no. Right now, we can't even afford to do that.' He looked away. 'I didn't want to tell you this, but I've had to borrow money from the bank. A lot of money. And if I don't pay it back we could lose this house.'

'I didn't know things were . . . that bad.'

'I'm afraid they are, my love. And that's why I have to take this job. It's a chance to get us back on track. A chance I might never have again.'

'I see,' she whispered.

And she did see. But that didn't make it any easier. Dad going away for months on end. Jess stuck in some vile boarding school. For days she'd gone round in a dream, picking at her meals, avoiding her friends at school, lying awake for hour after hour at night and, more than once, weeping at the sheer unfairness of it all.

In the end it was TV that came to her rescue. She was watching an interview with an eighteen-year-old girl called Naomi from Peckham, just a few miles away, who'd got a part in a big musical that was about to open in the West End. Naomi had talked about her life and then danced a routine from the show. As she did so, Jess had felt something inside herself begin to shift.

'I went to this stage school out in the countryside,' Naomi was saying. 'It was a boardin' school, and at first I missed my mum and dad, but when I settled in I made like these really, really good friends. And after that . . .'

'Yes?' prompted the interviewer.

A faraway look came into Naomi's eyes. 'After that it was great,' she said. 'We worked hard, all the singin' and dancin' and that, but we had the *best* time.'

'And which school was this?'

'It was called Arcadia,' said Naomi.

Jess watched the programme from beginning to end, and the next day watched it again online. When she was younger, she had dreamt about going to stage school, but even though she knew she was a good singer and dancer, it had seemed an impossible idea – out of her reach. No one she'd ever met had been to stage school. It was the sort of thing that people did in books and films – often before becoming pop stars. Not something that was open to ordinary people like her.

But the dream had never really gone away. It had lingered, waited for its moment, become a backbeat to her thoughts. And seeing Naomi from Peckham, who seemed ordinary enough with her toothy smile and her sing-song Jamaican accent (and who was a good dancer but not an *impossibly* good dancer), the idea had clicked smoothly and inevitably into place. If Naomi could go to stage school, then so could Jess! And suddenly nothing else would do. She was not only determined to go to stage school; she was determined to go to *that* stage school. Arcadia. The one where Naomi had been so happy.

Peter Bailey had been struck by the change in Jess that followed this decision. She suddenly seemed bright-eyed and wide awake again. And she was smiling. 'Stage school,' he said. 'Wow!' And then he'd frowned. 'Supposing you don't get in? Suppose they're all, I don't know, *full*. Or suppose you're not –'

'Dad, I'll get in, OK. Whatever it takes. To Arcadia. I've decided.'

'But you've never even –'

'Dad, that's where I want to go, OK? You go to Saudi Arabia, I'll go to Arcadia. Deal?'

Peter Bailey nodded. He knew better than to argue with his daughter when she had that look on her face. 'Deal,' he said.

And now here she was, with the wind in the trees and her new friends asleep around her. It had been hard to get into Arcadia, and it would be harder to stay here, but for the moment, here she was. And so was that boy. Dreamily, hugging every last detail to herself, Jess replayed his words, his smile, and that last meaningful wink. Perhaps she should start listening to Radiohead. And with this thought, finally, Jess closed her eyes.

5

The ballet studio was in the main school building, on the first floor. Vast and airy, it had once been a ballroom. Gilt-framed mirrors stood against the walls, and a dusty light streamed through the tall, uncurtained windows. The floor was of unvarnished wood and at the far end of the studio, beneath a chandelier, an elderly man was seating himself at an upright piano piled with musical scores. There were about two dozen girls waiting to take Miss Pearl's class, most of them wearing tracksuit bottoms over their tights. Some of them were warming up, stretching their leg muscles at the barre or lowering themselves into the splits on the floor, while others stood in groups chatting.

For a long moment, intimidated, Jess looked around her. This was a long way from the Norwood church hall with its clanking radiators. It all looked so . . . serious. *I should be stretching*, she thought. She hadn't done a class for a fortnight and suspected that she was going to be pretty sore by the end of the morning.

But she couldn't find the right ballet shoes. She rummaged again through the jumble of leg warmers and T-shirts in her bag, and realized with despair that she had left her comfortable, worn-in shoes in her suitcase in Room 10. Instead she had brought a brand-new pair, which, until they were properly broken in, would pinch her feet and give her blisters. Was there time to make it to the dorm building and back before class? She glanced at the clock. Four minutes to nine. If she ran . . . Quickly pulling on her track top, Jess marched to the door, only to meet a trim, bright-eyed figure moving in the opposite direction.

'So, Jessica. How are we today?'

'Er, we're fine, Miss Pearl.'

'Excellent. Well, chop-chop then. Shoes on.'

Returning to her bag, Jess took off her track top, pulled out the new shoes and jammed them on to her feet. As expected, they were painfully tight. She tried to wriggle her toes but couldn't. Around her, the others were taking their places at the barre. Despairingly, she slipped in between a couple of girls in front of one of the windows.

Clapping her hands for silence, Miss Pearl nodded at the pianist and they were off. From the beginning, the pace of the class was fast. Miss Pearl set the exercises once only and expected them to be remembered. Soon, despite the morning chill, Jess was sweating.

When they had finished the barre work, they moved to the centre of the studio and Miss Pearl divided the class into four groups. Having learnt the first routine, a series of speedy little jumps, Jess was able to watch the other students. There were a few who really struggled, and an equally small handful who clearly found the whole thing as easy as breathing. Annoyingly, the hateful Shannon Matthews was one of these. She had put her hair up into a neat blonde bun – a striking contrast to Jess's own mousy bird's-nest – and was wearing a floaty white chiffon skirt over her regulation dark-blue school tights. She looked good, Jess was forced to admit. Cool and willowy. To either side of her, equally streamlined, were her two best friends, Kelly Wilkinson and Flick Healey. *Just keep clear of them*, Ash had warned.

Jess was in the third group. She started the jumps confidently enough, but she couldn't straighten her toes inside the new shoes and landed heavily. 'Heels *down*, Jessica,' snapped Miss Pearl, but it was no good; Jess couldn't get the rhythm and finished the exercise with a series of graceless thuds. Limping to the edge of the studio, she pulled off her shoes, gasping with relief. 'What size are you?' whispered Ash, appearing beside her. 'I've got some spare fives.'

'Wow, thanks,' breathed Jess. 'These are killing me.' In fact she was a four and Ash's shoes were too loose for her, but she pulled them on anyway, looking up just in time to see Spike finish the exercise.

Jess stared. If Shannon was good, Spike was amazing, her long legs launching her effortlessly into the air and her arms describing beautiful lines against the light. To see her perform even the simplest movement was to know that she had been born to dance. It was as if she had been pre-programmed; as if every leap and turn was already there, imprinted into brain and muscle, waiting for its moment.

'Awesome, isn't she?' whispered Ash. 'I'd give anything to be able to move like that.'

Jess nodded, a little shaken by Spike's extra-ordinary talent. If she practised for a thousand years, she knew, she would never achieve the other girl's effortless fluency. But she could try. Concentrating harder than ever before, she made it through the next few routines without a mistake. Finishing the last of the pirouette exercises in a spray of sweat, she sank back against the barre and took a sip from her water bottle.

Beside her, Ash was doing the same. 'Looks like we've got company,' she murmured, swivelling her eyes towards the long window looking out on to the corridor. Outside, two figures were watching them. One, Jess saw, was The Boy, in a black T-shirt. The other had scruffy blond hair, and a towel slung round his shoulders. Both were grinning, their lips moving soundlessly beyond the glass window.

Glancing at them, her heart thumping painfully behind the scoop of her leotard, Jess raised an eyebrow at Ash.

'Johnny Finn and Zane Johnson,' Ash whispered. 'Double trouble, you might say.'

'I see,' murmured Jess, though she didn't really. Something about Johnny's mocking grin, though, made her want, very badly, to impress him. Taking her place for the next exercise, a series of split leaps, she took a deep breath in preparation.

'One and a *two*,' sang Miss Pearl as the pianist pounded out the familiar chords of *Swan Lake*. 'Three and a *four* . . . Good, Jessica.'

Miss Pearl was right. Jess's first two leaps were pretty good, and for those split seconds in the air, arms and legs outstretched, she felt as if she was flying. It was on the third that she came to grief. The borrowed shoes were just too big, and as she landed she felt her foot slip beneath her. She landed, as she had the day before, fair and square on her bum. Right on the bruise, in fact. It hurt so much that tears sprang to her eyes, and she curled up on the floor as the next wave of dancers came skimming towards her.

'Jessica, can I request that you sort out your footwear issues in time for tomorrow's class?' asked Miss Pearl acidly as Jess trailed painfully back to the barre. She nodded and, looking up at the window, saw that Johnny and Zane were laughing. Even worse, somehow, was the look of quiet triumph on Shannon's face.

6

'Seriously, don't worry about it,' said Ash as the three of them changed back into their day clothes in Room 10. 'I'm all over the place when it comes to ballet. It's no big deal. I mean, it's not like we're going to become ballerinas. Except for Legs here, of course,' she said, nodding at Spike.

'I know,' said Jess. 'I just would have liked my first class to have gone a bit better, that's all.' And above all, she thought, for Johnny Finn not to have seen her fall over again. It hurt that he'd laughed, but it hadn't surprised her. He must think she was a total ditz.

'Well, put it this way, things can only get better, right?'

'I guess,' said Jess, pulling down the top of her tights and angling round so that she could see her bruise in the mirror. It was the size of her fist, and a purplish colour.

'Yikes,' said Ash, wincing. 'That looks sore . . . Look, don't let La Perla scare you, OK? She's just trying to toughen you up. You obviously know your stuff, ballet-wise. You'll do fine, trust me.'

Looking up, Jess caught Spike's eye. Smiling, Spike nodded and gave her a thumbs up.

'Thanks, guys,' said Jess. 'I . . .'

Her words trailed off because at that moment the door swung open, Ash shrieked, and a huge grin split Spike's face.

The figure in the doorway looked around her with a flick of her silky red mane. 'So! Miss Nash! Princess! I see you've started the term without me again.' She hugged both of them, then turned a pair of amused green eyes on Jessica. 'And you must be the newbie. Welcome to the monkey house.'

'This is Jess,' said Ash. 'She poured puréed spinach into Shannon's hair within two hours of arriving here.'

'Wow. Good job, Jess. I'm Eleanor, but everyone calls me Foxy.'

'Hi there,' said Jess, trying to think of something interesting to say to this terrifyingly self-assured but apparently friendly creature. 'Did you . . . have an OK journey?'

'Nightmare,' said Foxy, dragging her suitcase into the room and collapsing on to the unused bed. 'I came up by train and it turned out that my mother had bought some kind of, I don't know, *budget ticket*-type thing, so I got asked to leave first class. I ended up in this compartment full of criminals, basically.'

'What kind of criminals?' asked Jess, wide-eyed.

'Oh, you know, criminal *types*,' said Foxy vaguely. 'Fat men in tracksuits, tattooed mums, children with food on their faces, that sort of thing.'

'You poor thing,' said Ash. 'How you must have suffered.'

'Well, yeah! The sooner I'm famous and whisked everywhere by helicopter, the better.'

'And Miss Allen? What'll you say? About being back late, I mean.'

'Oh, I'll tell her something,' said Foxy, sticking one leg in the air and inspecting her high-heeled shoe. 'Fact is this awesome new club opened last night and *everyone* was going. What was I supposed to do?'

There was a short silence, and then Ash looked at her watch. 'We'd better get down to the study block, guys.'

Foxy winced. 'I hate academic studies. What've we got first?'

'Geography,' said Ash, glancing at her timetable.

'Oh please,' groaned Foxy. 'Get a satnav.'

7

Six hours later, Jess lay on her bed, her mind a whirl and her body aching. As well as the morning's ballet class, they'd done several academic classes, an acting improvisation session and an hour's voice exercises.

Johnny was in her improv class, and he was clearly a smart and inventive actor. When it came to Jess's turn, she and a girl named Emma Tucker had been asked to create a scene at a party. Emma had to greet her as a long-lost friend, while Jess had to hide the fact that she hadn't the faintest idea who the other girl was. The exercise had gone more or less OK, and Johnny had given her a grin and a thumbs-up, but Jess hadn't forgiven him for laughing at her in ballet class, so she'd pretended not to notice.

Her eyes half closed, she registered the faint creak of bedsprings as Spike turned the pages of a magazine a couple of metres away. From the other side of the room came the rattle of the electric kettle and an unhurried shudder of drawers as Foxy unpacked.

'Sugar, Jess?' Ash asked.

'Mmm, please . . .' Blinking, she raised herself on one elbow, and then remembered. 'Actually, no. I won't.' Since that morning, and the sight of herself in the ballet-studio mirror – not overweight, exactly, but hardly whippet-thin – she had resolved to eat and drink sensibly. Or try to.

'OK, one good intention coming up . . .'

Jess sipped her tea. Outside the window, there was a sudden flapping of wings as a pigeon came to roost in one of the trees.

'Have you got a boyfriend, Jess?' Foxy asked, stuffing a pink mohair sweater into a drawer.

'Er, no,' said Jess. 'No, I haven't.'

'Now you're supposed to ask Foxy if she's got one,' prompted Ash, lifting a tea bag from her mug by its string. 'And she'll tell you yeah, like, *loads*.'

'As it happens, I am currently unattached,' said Foxy, forcing the drawer shut with her knee. 'I won't pretend that there weren't one or two romantic moments over the holidays, but basically I'm rather off boys at the moment. They're just too needy and time-consuming. So right now I'm having a me month. Giving the love to the one who deserves it most.'

'What about you, Ash?' asked Jess. 'Are you going out with anyone?'

Ash laughed. 'I think my dad would shoot any boy who came within a mile of our house.'

'What about Zane?' Foxy asked. 'How's that coming along?'

For a moment there was a faraway look in Ash's eye. 'Like I said, my parents . . .'

'Do you always do what your parents want?' asked Jess.

'She's their princess,' explained Foxy. 'The princess of Basingstoke.'

'As it happens, I *am* a princess in Ghana.'

Foxy rolled her eyes. 'Honestly, Ash . . .'

'But I am,' said Ash plaintively. 'Why does no one believe me?'

'Because we've met your parents, sweet thing, and your dad's an orthodontist from Hampshire, not the king of Ghana.'

'I keep telling you, it doesn't . . . Oh, forget it. Just forget it.' She turned to Jess. 'My mum, right. I wore these low-rider jeans to the cinema this one time – I was just with a couple of girlfriends, no guys – and she's like: "Ashanti, are you *really* planning on going out like that? I can see six full inches of belly, girl, and it is *not* a pretty sight."'

'Looks OK to me,' smiled Jess.

'Yeah, well, I'm not saying that I couldn't lose an ounce or two. But that's not what she meant. You know mums.'

'Not really,' said Jess. 'My mum left.'

For a moment no one moved. Then Spike looked round, sharp concern in her eyes.

'What happened?' asked Foxy, still facing the chest of drawers.

'She went to South Africa to live with a guy called Derrick. A physiotherapist.'

'I'm sorry,' said Ash. 'That's just awful. Do you mind . . .?'

Jess shrugged. 'No. There isn't that much to tell. A car ran into the back of ours at a traffic light, and Mum got whiplash. She kept on getting neck pain and went to see a specialist at the hospital, who referred her to Derrick. She went for sessions twice a week, on Mondays and Wednesdays. And then, just before I went back to school after the Easter holidays, she told us. The two of them were off. To start a new life together in Durban.'

'Oh my *God*!' breathed Ash. 'How did your dad take it?'

'He was . . . you know, completely . . .' She closed her eyes.

'And they went?' asked Foxy.

'They went. The idea was that Derrick was going to open some sports-injury clinic. He told her that he had money and property out there. But it turned out there wasn't any money and the property was a house that belonged to his mother. So there were complications straight away, and it wasn't long before Mum was paying most of the bills out of her savings.'

Ash winced. 'She should've walked out.'

'Well, yeah. Dad sent her email after email. *Just come back, and we'll make a fresh start.* But she wouldn't. She wanted a divorce and she wanted Derrick. And in the end she got both.'

'So what's he like?' asked Foxy.

'I just met him once. He was weirdly tanned and had these creepy eyebrows.'

'Like the guy in *The Devil Wears Prada*?' asked Foxy.

Jess nodded, and Foxy shook her head. 'Those guys are the worst. D'you still see her?'

'To begin with she came back every few months. We'd go out, she'd tell me how bad she felt about going but she needed space to breathe, a life of her own, blah, blah, blah . . . And I'd tell her don't worry, Mum, I'm doing OK, moving on, whatever. But recently – I guess it's the money – she hasn't been coming so often . . .'

'So when did you last see her?'

‘About a year ago.’ She shrugged limply, and Spike took two long steps across the room and closed her arms round her in a silent hug.

‘So it’s just you and your dad,’ said Foxy.

Jess nodded. ‘Basically, yeah. Except that he’s now in Saudi Arabia. So all that’s kind of long-distance too.’

‘You’ve got us,’ said Ash. ‘And we’re right here.’

‘I know,’ said Jess. Afraid that she was going to cry, she looked very hard out of the window. ‘Sorry. I’m not very good at people being nice to me. I think I might just . . . go outside for a bit. Go for a walk.’

Spike hesitated for a moment, then followed her out of the room. The two of them made their way along the corridor, down the stairs and out into the summer evening.

‘You didn’t have to come,’ said Jess. ‘Really, I’m OK.’

But her new friend just smiled, and they strolled down the gravel drive together. Jess felt a stab of guilt at having shared so much private stuff with the others, but at the same time felt better for having done so. *I’m sorry, Mum*, she thought. *I know you just wanted to be happy. But weren’t we enough?*

Near the gates they peeled off to the right, across the lawn. From the smell of the grass, Jess guessed that it had been mown just a day or two earlier. The lawns were encircled by a shadowy ring of trees, with a narrow path snaking through, and for a while the two of them just walked. There were other students there, some with iPod wires trailing from their ears, lost in their music; others chatting and laughing in small groups. From the other side of the lawn the faint beat of rap music and distant shouts of encouragement were carried on the still summer air. Further away, someone was practising her scales, holding the highest notes with a bird-like trill.

As they made their way along the path, which was splashed with evening sunshine, Spike pointed to the trailing branch of a giant chestnut tree. Grabbing hold of it, she pulled herself up and began to climb. If she was going to keep up, Jess saw, she'd have to follow. It took her three goes to haul herself on to the branch, which then swung scarily beneath her. Slowly, her heart pounding, she began to follow Spike.

Soon, she was . . . what? Five metres from the ground? Six? High enough to break her neck if she fell, anyway. *Don't look down*, she told herself. *Don't look down!* This was definitely the maddest, most dangerous thing she'd ever done.

And then something strange happened. She stopped being frightened. She was enclosed, on all sides, by green leaves and by the creamy, pink-flecked flowers that rose like candles from the outer boughs. A metre or so above her Spike was comfortably supported in the fork of a branch. Finding a branch of her own, Jess planted her feet against the silver-grey trunk and lay back. Extraordinarily, she felt safe. The rap music whispered through the air, and she could hear the faint whooping as the break-dance crew rehearsed their spins and freezes.

'This is weird,' she said.

Spike smiled and pointed. On the flat roof of the dormitory block, two hundred metres away, three boys were sitting against the parapet. A fourth was climbing a fire-escape ladder to join them. Above their heads, Jess could see a faint haze of cigarette smoke.

'Boys are so gross,' said Jess and, seeing Spike's arched eyebrow, smiled. 'You know what I mean,' she added.

Spike nodded.

'Is there someone you like?' Jess asked.

Spike grinned, giving nothing away. A breeze shivered the pale-green chestnut leaves. Then she pointed to the school and back at Jess, with an enquiring look on her face.

'Why did I want to come here?' Jess asked.

'Do you want to dance? To sing? To act?' Spike hadn't actually spoken, but the language of her hands and arms and fingers was so clear that she might as well have done.

Now it was Jess's turn to be silent. The truth was she wanted to be in a world in which people did all of those things as a matter of course. Where instead of rushing for a bus every morning and sitting in an office all day (she didn't have a very clear idea of what people actually did in offices, but she was sure it had to be really, really boring), people lived colourful, glamorous lives, dashing between theatres and TV studios and film sets and photo shoots. She imagined herself wearing a . . . well, ultra-fashionably dressed, anyway, hurrying out of a stage door into a blaze of camera flashes, and seeing people reaching out to her with autograph books, calling her name. And beyond them, beckoning to her, a dark-haired figure with ice-blue eyes . . . The vision faded. Spike was looking at her as if she could read her mind, and for a moment Jess felt embarrassed. It wasn't, she knew, a very realistic dream. 'Right now,' she said. 'I just want to . . .'

She was going to say that she just wanted to stay at Arcadia, but she didn't quite get the second half of the sentence out because, on the dormitory roof, two further figures had climbed the fire-escape ladder to join the others. One was Shannon

– even at two hundred metres Jess could recognize the catwalk-model figure and the honey-blonde hair – and the other, just as unmistakably, was Johnny Finn. And they were kissing.

8

'G'night,' yawned Foxy.

The others mumbled their goodnights, and Spike waved sleepily. From outside the window, Jess heard a distant sigh. For the first couple of nights she had strained her ears after this sound, which had reminded her of her mum, and of her father's sadness, but now she knew that it was just the breeze in the trees.

I don't care about Johnny Finn, she told herself as the whispery quiet of the night washed over her. *As a friend or as anything else. I've only been here a few days, and we haven't exchanged more than half a dozen words . . . And that dance class, oh my* God*! What gives him the right to laugh at me like that? He's probably totally horrible; in fact he's* definitely *totally horrible. Must be, to fancy Shannon. How* could *he?*

All too easily, another part of herself answered. Shannon might be totally evil, but she was probably quite fanciable if you didn't care about the total evil. And boys never cared about that sort of stuff. In fact they liked it, which was partly why they were so gross themselves, right?

Whatever, she told herself. *From now on, it's all about working on my acting, singing and dancing. If I'm going to stay at this school, I simply don't have time for boys.*

Marching to the front of the studio, Foxy fixed the twenty-odd students with her long green eyes, and waited until there was absolute silence.

It was Jess's first class with Mr Huntley, head of singing, and the song that they all had to perform in turn was called 'Dying for You' – a big hit a year or two earlier for a band called Swift. Foxy's voice was low and smoky, and it struck Jess that she was barely singing at all. Just voicing the words, swinging her red hair and smiling that Foxy smile. She got about halfway through the song before Mr Huntley cut her off.

'OK, Eleanor, that'll do. A hundred per cent for presentation, as usual, and a big fat zero for technique. Ashanti, would you please show us how it's done?'

With an elegant shrug – she and Mr Huntley were old enemies – Foxy walked back to her place, and Ash stepped to the front. Ash was as confident as Foxy but the difference was that Ash could sing.

Really sing. She had a powerful rhythm-and-blues voice that, without any apparent effort, soared from a tigerish growl to top notes of crystal purity. 'Dying for You' wasn't such a great song, but Ash made it sound as if it was.

Looking round the studio, Jess was now able to put a name to quite a few of the students there. Of the girls, she knew Foxy and Ash, Shannon and her two sidekicks, Flick and Kelly (whom she had privately nicknamed the Resident Evils), a ballet-mad trio named Poppy Rattigan, Paige Purkiss and Georgie Maxwell (known to everyone as 'the Bunheads'), and chestnut-haired Emma who she'd done the improv scene with. Among the boys, she recognized Zane Johnson, who was Ash's on–off boyfriend (more off than on, Jess sensed), and a funny, lean-featured guy named Olly Francis, who seemed to get on with everyone. Both Zane and Olly were actors.

Unfortunately, Jess didn't know any of them well enough, Foxy and Ash excepted, to feel the least bit relaxed at the thought of singing in front of them. None of the Bunheads had much of a voice, so they'd be willing her on, and Olly looked like a supportive sort of guy. But Shannon and her gang would certainly be hoping that she made a fool of herself, and she suspected that Zane was more than ready to laugh at her efforts, too. At least Johnny wasn't in the class. That would have been too much.

Finally the dreaded moment came. Walking to the front, Jess stuck her hands in the back pockets of her jeans, grinned hopefully, and started to sing.

'There are times in my life when I feel so alone,
When I reach out to touch you and no one is there . . .'

For a moment, Jess caught Foxy's eye and saw the other girl smile encouragingly.

'I've been hoping and hoping you'll pick up your phone,
and I'm starting to wonder if you really care . . .'

Deep breath. Change of key.

'I'm dying for you, yes I'm dying for you,
I'm hurtin' so bad I don't know what to do . . .'

Caught up in the song, Jess pulled her hands from her pockets. Unfortunately, not just her hands came out. With them came an old bus ticket and a couple of meal vouchers from the dining hall, which fluttered slowly to the floor. A tiny snort of laughter came from the left-hand side of the studio, where Shannon was standing with Kelly and Flick. It wasn't much, but it was enough to send Jess's voice veering off-key. Self-conscious, furious with herself, she ground to a halt. After a moment she tried to start the song again, but it sounded worse. 'Never listen to yourself singing,' her teacher at home used to say.

Somehow she struggled through to the end. Alongside the annoyance at having messed the song up was the realization that her phone wasn't in her pocket. Had she left it on her bed? No, it had been in her pocket this morning, she was sure. Damn. Still, it had her name on it in indelible marker. Like her dad had insisted.

'Well done!' whispered Olly as she crept back to her seat. He was definitely unusual-looking, with his red-gold hair and intense grey eyes, but his smile was kind.

'I was *awful*!' breathed Jess.

'You made it through,' murmured Olly. 'That's what counts.'

'Oliver, when you and Jessica have finished your conversation . . .'

Olly moved confidently to the front. Naturally, he had a brilliant voice, and his rendition of the song was both witty and touching. *Oh God*, thought Jess, *I am* so *the odd one out here. I should just leave now.* And then, happily, it was Poppy Rattigan's turn, and she was so hopelessly flat that she made Jess sound positively professional. But then very few of the students had an exceptional talent for both singing and dancing, Jess had noticed. Most tended to favour one over the other.

There had been a time when Jess had thought of herself as a bit of an all-rounder, but this first week at Arcadia had put her right on that score. What was good in an after-school class at the local church hall didn't cut much ice in this sort of company. Poppy Rattigan could afford to laugh at her own singing because she was an accomplished ballet dancer and a real beauty – slender and violet-eyed. Like Foxy and Shannon, she had the supercharged confidence of those who knew they only had to walk into a room to have everyone staring at them.

Compared to these birds of paradise, Jess felt very ordinary indeed. Even her hair let her down. Everyone else seemed to have fabulous hair, from Emma Tucker's chestnut waves to Spike's all-attitude crop, to the Resident Evils' silky blonde tresses (which were the sort you could twist up with a finger, poke a pencil through, *et voilà* – total cocktail chic!).

Jess's hair was a mid-brown colour and the sort

that frizzed up the moment a comb went anywhere near it. The only shampoo she'd ever found which really controlled it had been in the bathroom of her aunt's flat in Mitcham. She'd used it for a week, with excellent results, before finding out that it was meant for dogs. Shapewise, Jess felt pretty ordinary too. She knew how to make the best of herself – basically, tight black jeans – but she'd heard Shannon dismissively refer to someone having 'a civilian's body', and she'd been pretty sure Shannon had been talking about her.

After the singing class, she was walking back to the dorm block to look for her phone, when she became aware that someone had fallen into step beside her. It was Olly.

'You know, you could sing really well if you gave yourself half a chance,' he began.

'Not!' said Jess bitterly. 'Like I said, I was *awful*.'

'Will you let me help you?'

'Olly, it's nice of you, but I kind of think I'm beyond help right now.'

He smiled. 'Just five minutes. Give it a try.'

'Why do you . . . want to help me?'

'Because, although this might seem a bit weird, we do try to help each other here at Arcadia. At least us human beings do.'

'But not the aliens, huh?'

'No. The aliens make it their business to make everyone else feel just as bad as they possibly can. But wherever you go there'll always be people like that. So you might as well get used to it.'

'I s'pose you're right.'

'I am right. Believe me. Now are we ready to give that song another go?'

Jess looked around her. They were on the edge of the woods by the school wall and there wasn't anyone nearby. And bursting into song at a moment's notice was one of the things that people seemed to do here.

'OK,' she said, a little hesitantly.

He ran long fingers through his red-gold hair. 'The trick, I find, is to concentrate on the meaning of the words, rather than the words themselves. So when you sing *There are times in my life when I feel so alone*, think of a time like that. Think of a time when you really have felt . . . Oh my goodness, Jess, are you crying?'

She was, and it was the words of that stupid song which had set her off. 'Sorry,' she muttered, rubbing her eyes furiously. 'Didn't mean to . . .'

'Wait, I've got a tissue somewhere,' he said, searching his pockets. 'Here.'

She reached out for it, but blinded by tears, managed only to dig him in the ribs.

'It's OK. Don't move.' Carefully, he wiped her

cheeks, and then placed the soggy tissue in her hand.

'Thank you,' she sniffed. 'I'm sorry, it's just . . .'

'I know. This place can all get a bit much at times. Been there myself, on occasion.'

'Really?' she ventured, noisily blowing her nose.

'Really. Dramas like you wouldn't believe.'

'I'm not sure I believe that,' she said, sniffing.

'Everybody has their bad-weather days, Jess. Trust me. It comes with the territory.'

'I guess so.'

'I know so, girlfriend. Now blow your nose and let's sing. Follow me . . . *When I reach out to touch you and no one is there . . .*'

Jess joined in. Uncertainly at first, and then letting her feelings guide her. And it sounded OK. Somehow, with Olly, she didn't care if she made a fool of herself. Other people were watching them, but she no longer cared about that either. She was just one more student singing in the school grounds.

'Thanks,' she said, when she'd finally belted straight through the song on her own, pretty much note-perfect. 'You really, *really* helped.'

Olly shrugged. 'You're a pretty good singer, you know. You just needed to chill out. Defrost a bit.'

'Hang on a minute,' she said, laughing. 'That doesn't make sense.'

'This is Arcadia,' said Olly, with a half-smile that made him look, somehow, much older than he was. 'It doesn't have to make sense.'

9

Climbing the stairs to Room 10 before lunch, Jess met Spike coming the other way, her bag trailing pointe-shoe ribbons. From her friend's earphones, Jess could hear the whisper of a Shakira song

'Your phone,' signed Spike, pointing back upstairs.

'Someone's found it? Brilliant – thanks, Spike.'

The phone was on her bed, and Jess pocketed it with relief. It was clunky and unfashionable, but it held her whole life.

'Hanging out with Olly Francis, I see,' said Ash, checking her reflection in the mirror.

'Er, yeah. He seemed friendly. Isn't he?'

'I don't know him that well. He's one of the actor crowd. But nice enough, I guess.'

'He's kind,' said Jess. 'He helped me with my singing.'

'Ah,' said Ash, with the hint of a smile. 'I see.'

'Isn't he gay?' murmured Foxy, scrolling through

her touch-phone menu with long, manicured nails.

'Oh please!' said Ash. 'You think everybody's gay.'

'Not everyone,' said Foxy, yawning. 'Just the few who don't fancy me.' Staring at the phone, she suddenly yelped: 'Yay! That's so *cool* . . .'

'Tell,' said Ash.

'When we're all together,' said Foxy with a secretive grin. 'Let's do lunch.'

Spike was waiting at their usual table, picking at a cheese and tomato salad. When she saw Foxy, she lifted her hands and fluttered her fingers in a quick question.

'Yes,' said Foxy. 'I've just heard. The answer is yes.' She turned to the others. 'As I told Spike earlier on, a friend of my parents is making a film with – wait for it – Alex Karman and Rachel Manners . . .'

'Alex Karman!' Ash breathed. 'He is *soooo* awesome.'

'. . . And they're filming near London in a few weeks' time. There's a chance we might be able to, like, be in a couple of the scenes.'

'Doing?'

'Walk-on parts. That sort of thing. Nothing enormous, but . . .' She turned to Jess. 'You're included too, obviously.'

'Wow, cool!' said Jess. 'Thanks. But is it . . . I mean will Miss Allen . . .?'

'Miss Allen doesn't need to know anything about it,' said Foxy firmly.

'But supposing she finds out?' wailed Ash. 'We will be *so* expelled. And there've gotta be rules about fourteen-year-olds working on films. Aren't we supposed to have, like, chaperones or something?'

'Chill,' said Foxy, poking at her mashed potato with distaste. 'No one ever got anywhere in show business by obeying the rules. And you know the best thing – apart from Alex falling instantly in love with all of us, of course? Shannon Matthews and her crew will be totally and absolutely wiped-out jealous. They'll be gutted.'

'Cool,' said Jess, forcing a smile. But she wasn't so sure. Getting one up on Shannon and the Resident Evils was all very well, but being caught breaking school rules was another thing altogether. Talentless *and* a troublemaker. She'd be expelled so fast she'd –

'That's settled then,' said Foxy. 'I'll get Mum to fix it up with Regina, the director. I'm sure we won't need chaperones if we're just, like, visiting the set. Now what on earth is this hideous stuff they're expecting us to eat?'

Leaning forward, Spike began to mime a story,

Ash translating for Jess as she went. 'When I was little,' she began, 'we had a dog.' From her stroking movements, Jess could almost see it on the table, quivering beneath her touch.

'The dog used to steal my . . .' She shaped several miniature figures.

'Teddy bears?' suggested Ash.

'Barbie dolls?' said Foxy.

'Beanie Babies?' ventured Jess, and Spike nodded enthusiastically and grinned. 'He used to take them and hide them and' – sticking her finger down her throat – 'throw up all over them. So you'd just be going to bed, and you'd turn down the cover, and there would be this Beanie Baby on your pillow, covered in dog sick.'

'Thank you for that, Spike,' said Ash, laying down her fork. 'You really know how to stimulate a girl's appetite.'

As Spike smiled and bowed, Jess felt her phone vibrate in her jeans pocket. A text. Probably her dad, she thought, with a stab of guilt. Pulling out the phone below the table – no point in advertising its deep uncoolness – she thumbed the message button.

> I spy w my little eye . . .
> some1 fit!

A thump of alarm slammed into her chest. Who was watching her? And why? Heart pounding, she glanced round the dining hall, but no eyes met hers. And, as the shock and the slight creepiness of the message faded, a slow warmth spread through her. Someone in this place – this scary home of the beautiful and the talented – thought she was super-fit! Of course he was watching her. Everyone was watching everyone else here, weren't they?

'Look at this!' she said, handing her phone to Foxy.

Foxy rolled her eyes. 'Just some stupid guy who's got hold of your number. Delete it.'

Slightly regretfully, Jess did so. But Foxy was right. It could have been anyone.

10

After lunch there was an hour's break before sports, and Jess decided to go for a walk. The school was laid out more or less in the shape of a square. In front, facing the drive, was the main building, which was of red brick and looked quite old, with its arched doorways and its tall, spooky-looking tower.

The main building held the school offices, the dining hall, the classrooms, and the music and rehearsal studios. The ground floor was panelled in oak, with ancient, shined linoleum underfoot, and smelt faintly of furniture polish. Upstairs, there were the staff quarters and the large ballet studio.

If the main building was the front of the square, the sides were made up by the dorm blocks: the girls' on the left, and the boys' on the right. And at the back was the theatre, a vaulted Gothic building, which, at first sight, Jess had mistaken for a church. She'd been inside the theatre just once, and it had been a thrill to stand on the stage, with its dark floorboards, banks of overhead lights and faded velvet curtains.

The main building, dorm blocks and theatre enclosed a quadrangle, a covered walk around a square of lawn, and it was here that Jess took herself after lunch. As she left the dining hall, she checked that her phone was still switched on, in case her mystery admirer should decide to text her again.

The quad was deserted except for a knot of students in one corner, among whom Jess recognized Poppy and Paige. True to form, both of them were carrying dance bags and had their hair scraped back into buns. Two boys were leaning against the wall in the deliberately casual way that boys did when they wanted to impress girls. One was a tall second year she didn't know, and the other was Johnny.

'Hi, Jess,' said Paige brightly.

Johnny swung round, and Jess felt a kind of thrilled dread as the ice-blue eyes met hers.

'At last,' said the second year, pointing at her. 'Someone human!'

Jess glanced at him, not understanding. Johnny, meanwhile, just stared at her.

'So we're not human?' asked Poppy, clearly

irritated that Jess had distracted the boys from her and Paige.

'No way,' grinned the second year. 'You're from Planet Ballet.'

Jess wasn't so sure that she wanted to look human, right at that instant. It sounded like shorthand for messy-haired and big-bottomed. But looking at the two dancers, with their neat little heart-shaped faces and their endless sway-back legs, she had to admit that she probably didn't come from the same planet that they did.

Johnny took a step towards Jess, his half-smile suggesting that there was something that he wanted to say to her. Something that he wanted to explain. But somehow the moment passed and, ducking past the four of them, Jess made a speedy exit.

Is it always going to be like this at Arcadia? she wondered despairingly. Her on the outside, looking in? The ordinary girl among the extraordinary, always a step behind everyone else, never quite understanding what was going on?

What was up with Johnny? Whenever she saw him around the school, even though they'd barely spoken, she sensed a connection between them. A secret flicker of understanding. But, with Paige, Poppy and that guy there, it had all suddenly turned weird. Was it because she'd caught him out chatting up the girls, or was he trying to tell her something? That what they had was strictly between the two of them. Or the opposite – and her heart sank at the thought – that there was nothing between them at all?

In the north-eastern corner of the quad, a vaulted passage led between the theatre and the boys' dorm block to the back lawn and the woods. Nobody seemed to be in sight, and she continued in an unhurried diagonal across the grass. Overhead, the summer sky was a cloudless blue, and gradually, as she felt the sun's warmth on her hair, and on her shoulders and arms, her doubts and uncertainties began to lift.

I am just so amazingly lucky to have got into this place, she thought, *even if I do sometimes feel like an outsider. Because even if I haven't always known it, this is what I've always wanted. This strange, intense life where you pour your heart out day after day, and push your body till your feet blister and your muscles ache, but you keep going because there up ahead, shimmering like a mirage, is that other world. The world of performance, transformation and magic.*

Some day, Jess told herself fiercely, she would feel the applause break over her like a tidal wave. Some day she would see the credits roll, and there would be her name.

Following the mossy path through the woods, she wound in and out of the trees, beneath low canopies of beech and oak, and through patches of shade and sunshine. And then, quite suddenly, she found herself on the edge of a circular clearing.

It was an amphitheatre, cut out of the slope, with stepped rings of seating. The steps were stone, and mottled with yellowish lichen. The stage was a semi-circle of uncut grass. Jess stood for a moment, staring. There was something wild and mysterious about the place. Something almost pagan.

'Hand in hand, with fairy grace,
Will we sing, and bless this place . . .'

Jess whirled round. The voice, low and musical, seemed to come from everywhere and nowhere.

'That's how an amphitheatre works, you see. Like a kind of loudspeaker. Haven't you been here before?'

Jess could see her now. A slender black woman with her hair in an elegant up-do, wearing a long-sleeved T-shirt and pleated skirt, both in olive green. She was sitting, motionless, on the lowest step on the far side of the stage, and Jessica recognized her at once. Colette Jones, head of drama. Formerly of the Royal Shakespeare Company and the National Theatre, and considered by many the finest Cleopatra of her generation.

'No,' said Jess. 'I mean, I knew it was here in the woods somewhere. I've heard people talk about it.'

'And now you've found your way here.'

'Well, yeah . . . I guess.'

'Say after me: "Yes, I've found my way here."'

Jess tried to say the simple phrase as the teacher had, but it sounded hissy and breathy.

'Come here,' said Miss Jones, and Jess walked down to the semi-circular stage of the amphitheatre.

'Stand there. Back straight, supporting your voice. Now, say it again: "Yes, I've found my way here."'

Jess did so, and this time the words came out free and clear.

'All right, Jessica. Better. Now repeat after me:

'Come, my lord; and in our flight,
Tell me how it came this night . . .'

Jessica tried to repeat the words, surprised that the teacher knew her name, but this time her breathing got mixed up.

'In through the nose, out through the mouth,' said Miss Jones patiently. 'And take it slowly.'

Jess tried it again. The sound was better, but this time she forgot the second line.

'Again, Jessica:

'Come, my lord . . .'

Eventually, after half a dozen goes, she got it right.

'Now add the second couplet:

'That I sleeping here was found
With these mortals on the ground.'

Jess delivered all four lines, and suddenly it was easier. The words seem to float out low and clear, to hang in the air for a few seconds. Miss Jones looked at her for a moment, her expression unreadable.

'What are they from, those lines?' Jess asked, imagining the ranks of stone seats alive with spectators.

'Guess.'

'Really, I don't know.'

'No one's told you about the end-of-term performance?'

'Er, no. Well, I know there is one, but . . .'

'Every summer term, on Parents' Day, the first

years perform *A Midsummer Night's Dream*. It's an Arcadian tradition, and in my view a very good one.'

'Wow. Shakespeare! I didn't know.'

'Well, you know now,' said Miss Jones. 'Casting is announced in a couple of weeks' time, so you'd better get to work. Repeat after me:

'First, rehearse your song by rote,
To each word a warbling note . . .'

Jessica did so and, once again, the words seemed to hang in the air. 'Those lines . . .' she began questioningly.

'Titania. Queen of the fairies.' Miss Jones looked her straight in the eye. 'Would you like to be considered for the role?'

Jess nodded, a kind of weightless feeling spreading inside her. Right then, she could think of nothing in the entire world she wanted more.

'Well, so does every single other girl in your year, so you'd better pull your fairy socks up.'

'I will,' said Jess, the strange feeling still inside her. She was about to walk away, when a thought occurred to her. 'How do you know my name?' she asked, looking up to meet the teacher's gaze.

Colette Jones smiled her faint, unreadable

smile. 'You'd be surprised what I know,' she said. 'Now on your way with you. I've got some thinking to do, and here's where I do it best.'

Raising a hand, Jess backed away. In her pocket she felt the sudden, urgent vibration that meant a text message. Hurrying away, she put several twists of the path between her and the amphitheatre, and then pulled out her phone.

I spy w my little eye ;-)

Jess whipped round. This wasn't so funny. Surely no one could see her here in the woods. Uneasy now, she hurried back towards the main building.

11

The next Monday morning, shortly after breakfast, the sun slid behind a heavy bank of clouds and stayed there. The week that followed was grey and overcast, with sudden showers that left the trees dripping and the lawns sodden. In the big first-floor ballet studio there was a leak in the roof, and classes were conducted to the steady *plip-plip* of drops into a bucket alongside the chugging rhythms of the piano. A blanket-like chill seemed to settle over the school, and everywhere smelt of damp hair. It didn't feel like a summer term at all.

Every day, there was at least one new text on Jess's phone. All said more or less the same thing. That the texter was watching her, and that he fancied her. Jess wasn't quite sure why she didn't tell her room-mates she was still getting the texts, but she didn't, and after a time it was too late to say anything.

If she was being honest with herself, Jess knew

she didn't want to be told by the others that she was the victim of a wind-up. That some boy was leading her on, waiting for her to reply, so he could snigger about her with his mates. Much more exciting to think – all right, to pretend – that someone, somewhere, really did fancy her, really did think she was pretty and couldn't stop watching her. Someone like Johnny, perhaps?

She would have dwelt on the whole thing much more if she hadn't been so busy. But if she was to survive the first-term assessment she knew that she needed to work really hard. Her averages just had to come up. So she had thrown herself into her ballet and dance sessions, pushing herself until, despite the colourless skies outside, the sweat ran into her eyes. She'd worked equally hard at her singing, practising her scales and trying to deliver confident, heartfelt performances in Mr Huntley's classes.

But her efforts didn't seem to get her anywhere. In ballet, no matter how hard she tried, she just couldn't get off the ground. Her pointe shoes seemed to stick to the floor, so that she lurched from step to step as if she was dancing through glue. In singing, her voice seemed to vanish into the damp air. It was as if the place – Arcadia itself – was telling her that she wasn't good enough. Whether her teachers noticed how hard she was trying, she wasn't sure. Sometimes it seemed to her that they looked away whenever she was dancing, or deliberately missed her out when it was her turn to deliver Eponine's speech from *Les Misérables*, or to sing 'I'm Not That Girl', from *Wicked*.

One afternoon Jess flipped open her laptop to find an email from her mother.

Darling J,

How are you, and how is life at your lovely stage school? You must feel like the luckiest girl in the world! As you know I dreamt of a life in Showbiz and everyone said that I had Great Talent, especially for Tap, and one year I was one of the juveniles in *Aladdin* at the Connaught Theatre in Worthing. Your Aunty Rena was in the panto too but didn't have a dancing part, she was a jellyfish I think. I would have given anything to go to somewhere like Arcadia but it was not to be. So work hard, my darling, and become a star! Do it for me!

Your loving MUM

PS V. hot and dusty here. Flies everywhere. Will try to come over before too long. Missing you x

As always it was good to hear from her, and upsetting at the same time. It would be easier if she thought her mum was happy, but Jess was sure she wasn't, and this knowledge, together with the unlikelihood of her parents ever getting together again, cast long shadows through her thoughts.

Everyone was talking about *A Midsummer Night's Dream* now, and classes had suddenly become intensely competitive as everyone tried his or her best to impress teachers who might have a say in the casting. For the first time, Jess realized just how ruthless the business of performance was. If one person was to succeed, others had to fail. There was no way round it.

And right now it seemed likely that she was going to be the one doing the failing. Wherever she looked, and despite her best efforts, there was always someone better than her. Always someone who picked up the routine quicker, delivered the speech more expressively, held the high note longer. If only she had some special talent, like Spike with her dancing, Ash with her singing, or Foxy with that what-the-hell star quality that would surely get her whatever she wanted in life.

All three of them took it for granted that they would have big parts in the Parents' Day show, which was probably, thought Jess, why they had avoided mentioning it for so long. And perhaps there was another reason, which was that she –

Jess – almost certainly wouldn't get a big part. Might struggle, in fact, to get a part at all.

Not all of the teachers were ignoring her, though. Since meeting Colette Jones at the amphitheatre, Jess had seen her around the school a number of times. Sitting in on a voice-technique class, watching an improv session in the theatre, glancing through the window at one of Mr Roebuck's jazz classes. Jess sensed that Colette Jones was keeping a quiet eye on her. Which would have been great if she felt more confident about her abilities, but the slight, elegant figure of the teacher always seemed to appear at the exact instant when Jess was singing off-key or wrong-footing herself in some way.

Jess had the impression that Johnny was watching her too, but in a different way. She'd sense his presence and there he'd be, darting glances at her that were so fleeting, so barely there, that Jess sometimes wondered if she was imagining them. And there Shannon would be too, as often as not, her blue eyes wary, watching both of them.

Ignore it, Jess told herself. She'd go mad trying to figure those two out. There just wasn't the time. On top of everything else, she was teaching herself sign language to help her communicate with Spike. Right now she was working on fingerspelling, a way of making words using hand and finger movements. In a moment she was going down to join the others for dinner in the canteen. It was Friday, so there would be underdone fish fingers and watery broccoli. Yuck. Her phone buzzed in her pocket.

Like 2 meet?

As usual, the sender had concealed his number. Should she meet whoever it was? Should she even answer? Hurriedly, before she could change her mind, she thumbed out a reply.

Where?

Another buzz.

Quad

OK c u in 5

Well, she'd soon know who had been going to all this trouble.

Logging off from the fingerspelling site, zipping her school tracksuit up to her chin – it had been raining yet again – Jess glanced in the mirror. She looked pale, and her hair could do with a wash. Too bad. If she was as fit as this guy seemed to think she was, she didn't need to worry about such things.

Two minutes later she was making her way out of the lower door of the girls' dorm block and into the quad. After the rain, the sky was iron-grey. There were plenty of students in the stone-floored walkway, most of them hurrying towards the dining hall for dinner, but nobody seemed to be looking out for her especially. Then suddenly there was Johnny. He was with Zane and, though he looked briefly in Jess's direction, his eyes seemed to pass over her.

So, she thought, her heart sinking, *it's not him.* And if it wasn't him, then frankly, she wasn't interested. Slowly, not bothering to look around her now, she made her way to the dining hall. Before she'd even gone through the double doors, her nose told her that she'd been right. It was fish fingers and broccoli.

12

'OK,' said Foxy. 'I've finalized everything, so here's the plan.'

It was Wednesday evening, and the four of them were sitting in the flickering half-light of the dorm-block TV room. The set was ancient and wonky, but the TV room was a comfortable place to put your feet up after a day's classes, especially if, as today, it was wet outside. Right now, there was a wildlife show on BBC1, and a lioness had just sunk her fangs into the neck of a wildebeest, which, dazed with terror, was sinking to its knees.

'Oh yikes,' breathed Ash. 'Look at that poor animal.'

'Oh please!' said Foxy. 'It's appearing on TV, isn't it? Anyway, I know it's a few weekends away but here's what we're going to do, to get to the filming. We're going to get up at seven a.m. – yes, Spike, I did say *seven* a.m. – and get into our tracksuits, so that if anyone sees us leaving the building we're just going for an early-morning run. Yeah, I know that's unlikely, but there you go. Anyway, we do a lap or so of the school, then it's into the woods and over the wall and down to the T-junction, where a minicab's meeting us. And yes, I've booked it. So, minicab to the station, then train to Richmond, where the filming's happening. We can walk from Richmond Station.'

'How about the breakfast register?' asked Ash, a flutter of worry in her voice.

'Taken care of,' said Foxy. 'Georgie Maxwell's signing us in. I had to lend her my Miu Miu jeans, but she's taking care of it. Then we do the filming, dazzle Alex Karman, hang out with Rachel Manners and zap back in time for dinner. Easy-peasy!'

Spike nodded excitedly and Jess forced a smile, but inside she still wasn't so sure. First years were allowed to take the bus into Pangbourne or Henley-on-Thames on Saturdays, but London – and Richmond certainly counted as London – was strictly out of bounds. And she was pretty sure that doing unapproved film work was on the forbidden list too. If they were caught . . .

Ash echoed her fears. 'Guys, are you really, *really* sure this is the best idea?' she began. 'I mean, what are we hoping to get out of this?'

'Oh come on, Ash, listen to yourself,' said Foxy.

'An adventure! A bit of glamour! And, best of all, a day with Alex Karman. Of course it's risky, but all the most exciting things are.'

Ash looked at her for a second, grinned and nodded.

'And just wait until Shannon and her gang hear about it,' Foxy mused, a faraway look in her eye. 'They'll be off-the-scale jealous.' She turned to Jess. 'So are you in?'

Jess nodded. Foxy was right. Success meant seizing the moment. Taking your chances whenever they were offered. And, after all, who knew what a day's filming with Alex Karman might lead to? She looked up. On the TV screen, a praying mantis was eating her mate with a loud crunching sound. *Hello, Mum*, Jess thought.

'Yes,' she said. 'I'm in.'

13

On Friday morning, finally, they woke up to fine weather and a cloudless sky. For Jess, the day started with ballet class, which for once went well, earning her a thoughtful nod of approval from Miss Pearl. After lunch she spent an hour with Spike, practising her signing and fingerspelling.

She had received no more anonymous text messages, so it seemed as good a time as any to bring Spike up to date.

Bin gettin weird texts, she spelt out, and held out her phone so that her friend could read her inbox. At least a dozen messages were stacked up there, all with the sender's name withheld. Her frown deepening, Spike read through them one by one. At the end she turned to Jess and spread her hands questioningly.

'I know,' said Jess. 'I should have told you. I'm sorry. It's just . . . Well, I thought they might be from . . . from Johnny.'

Smiling, Spike placed her hand over her heart.

Jess nodded. 'I sort of do. It's stupid, I know. I mean, I don't really know him at all, and I know he's with Shannon, but whenever I see him, like in the dining hall or in improv classes, there just seems to be this connection between us. I'm not imagining it. I can feel him staring at me, and if I catch his eye he gives me these meaningful looks, as if we're sharing some deep secret.'

Spike considered what Jess had said, then called up the final message and showed it to Jess.

'I went,' said Jess. 'I went to the quad straight away. And there were lots of people there. But no one stopped or paid me any attention. Johnny was there but he just, like, stared straight through me, so it can't have been him.'

'Sounds like he's playing games,' Spike signed.

As the two of them glanced at each other, the phone buzzed and vibrated in Spike's hands, and she jumped.

'Whoo!' breathed Jess, taking the phone. 'That was spooky.'

See me now in the theatre
please – Colette Jones

Jess stared at the message, then showed it to Spike. 'I've never had a teacher text me before. I guess that's why they took all our numbers at the beginning of term.'

Spike glanced pointedly at the red-brick bulk of the theatre, with its weather-stained walls and towers.

'Yup, you're right, I'd better go. Laters.'

Spike nodded and reached into her pocket for her earphones.

To begin with, Jess couldn't see anything in the auditorium after the bright sunlight outside. On the stage, students were slowly moving scenery about, and after a short time she recognized Olly among them. Scanning the red-plush seats, she saw the slight, familiar outline of Colette Jones. Hesitantly, watching her step in the half-light, Jess descended the aisle until the two of them were level. Looking up, the teacher smiled and patted the seat next to her. A faint cloud of dust rose from the worn plush.

'Jessica, how are you?'

'I'm all right, Miss Jones, thanks.'

'Excellent.' She indicated the seat and Jess lowered herself into it, trying not to thump down too heavily. 'Now, I won't keep you too long because we both have much to do.' She inclined her head. 'I suppose what I really want to know is: how do you think you're getting on here? Is Arcadia everything you hoped for?'

'Er . . . yes. It's definitely everything I hoped it would be. It's wonderful. But . . .' Jess frowned and looked away.

'Go on.'

'I don't know. I'm just . . . really *bad* at everything. I'm trying, but . . .' She shrugged. 'It's all getting worse, not better.'

'That's how it feels, is it?'

Jess nodded and bit her lip.

'Would it surprise you to know that everyone who's ever been here – everyone with half an ounce of talent, that is – has felt exactly what you're feeling now?'

Jess stared at her, not trusting her voice.

'Hard though it is to believe, what you're going through is, quite simply, the process of learning and improving. It's painful because the old you has to go, to make way for the new. And that hurts.'

Jess nodded again.

'But it's necessary,' said the teacher quietly, laying a slender hand on Jess's arm. 'It has to happen if you're to get where you want to be. So just . . . soldier on, OK? Keep going.'

'OK,' whispered Jess.

'Now, the other reason I wanted to see you, is that I want you to learn the part of Titania.'

Jess felt her mouth fall open.

'I'm not making any promises, and I can't even guarantee you'll be an understudy, but learn it, OK?'

Terrified that she was going to cry, Jess took a deep breath. Nastiness she could just about deal with, but kindness got her every time. 'Thank you,' she breathed eventually. 'Thank you *so much.*'

'You won't thank me. It's a lot of work, and you probably won't get the chance to do it on stage. But I think it would be good for you.' Reaching into a bag at her side, Miss Jones took out a newly bound playscript and handed it to Jess. 'Now get lost. And get learning.'

14

Leaving the theatre, Jess felt as if she was walking on air, and as her face met the sunshine she closed her eyes, dazed by the brightness and the sheer brilliance of the chance that she had been given. Titania!

She would start immediately. Find a quiet place – in the woods, perhaps, that would be good – and imagine herself into the part. She had begun the walk back to the dorm block when her phone vibrated again. What now?

It was another text.

> **Sorry bout last time. Quad in 5.**
> **Promise 2 b there.**

No, thought Jess. *No! Not now. Not when I've . . .* She looked down at the neatly stapled script. More than anything, she wanted to read through it. To say the lines to herself and get the measure of the role. On the other hand, it was time to bring this whole silly text-message business to an end.

Thoughtfully, she made her way back towards the quad. If only she'd told the others. They'd have known exactly what to do. Jess thought of trying to find Spike, but she was probably dreaming the afternoon away in her chestnut tree.

The quad was deserted, apart from one very small junior girl who was scurrying towards the dorm block. Turning on her heel, really angry now, Jess was about to walk away when she heard a breathless voice behind her.

'Wait. Please. Don't go.'

Jess froze. She didn't have to look to know whose voice it was.

He came up behind her, his step wary, and then, as she turned, danced past her so that he was once more behind her.

'What d'you want?' she asked, her voice tight.

'To talk,' he said. 'Just that.'

'What've we got to talk about, exactly?'

'Shannon. Shannon and me. And you.'

'And can you give me one good reason why I'd want to talk to you about Shannon? Or anyone else, for that matter, given the way you've been stalking me?'

'Jess, that's not fair, I haven't been stalking you. Please, Jess, turn round. Look at me.'

She did as he asked and, despite her anger, her heart skipped a beat. He looked really worried, the ice-blue eyes meeting hers with something like desperation.

'So what do you call it then, when you pester someone with weird messages and totally, like, freak them out? What's that all about, Johnny?'

'OK, look, please. Let's just walk, and I'll tell you everything.'

'Tell me here.'

'I can't. You'll see why.'

She hesitated. He really did look very sorry for himself. 'Where then?'

His features relaxed a fraction of a degree. 'Just round the corner. The dorm block.'

'The boys' block? Are you kidding? You know girls aren't allowed in there.'

'You're allowed on the ground floor during the daytime.'

Jess hesitated again. Technically speaking, this was true, just as it was true that boys were allowed to visit the girls' block before 6 p.m. She'd never been inside the boys' block, though, and the idea didn't exactly thrill her. But what was the worst that could happen? If the ground floor of the boys' block was anything like the girls', it was just a hallway, a corridor and a common room with a couple of coffee-stained sofas. 'OK, I s'pose . . .'

He was already on the move, hurrying her, and he only seemed to relax when the dorm-block doors closed behind him. The boys' hall was shabbier than the girls', with a torn hip-hop poster and a cover shot of Rachel Manners Blu-tacked to the wall, and benches piled with clothes. It smelt, unmistakably, of teenage boys. Looking around it warily, as if seeing the place for the first time, Johnny shepherded Jess down the corridor into the common room, where several first years were kicking a dented Coke can backwards and forwards, attempting back-heels and other trick-shots. On their faces, Jess saw, was that look of rapt concentration that came over boys involved in completely pointless activities. One by one, they stopped and stared at her.

'Finn, my man, are you going to introduce us?' asked a tall, hawk-nosed guy whom Jess vaguely recognized from her maths set, as a second boy – fair hair, freckles, quite good-looking in a boy-band sort of way – turned down the drum-and-bass track which was thumping from a wall-speaker.

'Er, yeah, sure. This is Jess,' said Johnny and, with a nervous wince, steered her back out of the room. In the hall, he cleared a space for them on the bench among the track tops and sweatpants. 'OK,' he said. 'It's like this. Shannon and I are kind of an item, yeah?'

'So I hear,' said Jess coolly.

'I got with her last term.'

'Lovely for you both.'

'Well, yeah, up to a point. But the thing is this, and it's probably something you didn't know, but her parents are going through this like . . . *really* bad time. And I mean splitting-up bad.'

'That's awful,' said Jess quietly. 'I'm sorry for her.'

'Well, I'd understand if you weren't,' said Johnny. 'Given how she's been to you.'

'She doesn't like me, that's for sure. And, yeah, she has been pretty nasty. But that doesn't mean I'm glad that . . .' Jess shrugged. This whole parents-splitting-up thing wasn't a road that she wanted to go down. Certainly not with Johnny, here among the mouldy games kit.

'But you haven't wondered why she doesn't like you?'

'Where d'you want me to start? I'm new. An outsider. Not very confident, not very talented –'

'That is *so* not true,' said Johnny, and for a moment she just stared at him. The wild hair, the narrowed eyes, the upward twitch of his mouth towards his cheekbones . . .

'OK then. You tell me. Why did she pick on me?'

He leant forward, so that she couldn't see his

face. 'Because she sensed something. That I liked you.'

'But . . . you don't know me,' said Jess faintly.

'I know enough. I've seen how you've stood up to everything this place has thrown at you.'

'What, like you and Zane laughing at me through the dance-studio window? That sort of thing?'

He turned to her. 'That was just guy stuff, Jess. We weren't laughing at you. We were laughing at something else and just, like, *happened* to be looking at you. Which you'd better get used to, by the way, because it's gonna happen a lot.'

She stared at him, not quite believing him, but her heart was pounding all the same.

'Really, I wouldn't laugh at you, Jess. I think you're amazing. I really do.' He looked at her for a moment and then slowly, as if trying not to frighten a wild animal, extended his hand towards her face.

She couldn't move. It was as if an icy tide was rising inside her, at once thrilling and terrifying. And when his hand reached her, drawing softly down her cheek, her heart seemed to stop beating altogether. She closed her eyes, and he kissed her. It was the strangest feeling. Everything that she could see or hear seemed to fade away.

'*Whooo* . . . Finn, my man!'

'The Finnster strikes again!'

The voices seemed to come from far away, and then suddenly they were all round her. Pulling away from Johnny, she started to get up, but he took her arm and held it.

'Guys, please,' he said. 'Give us a break, yeah?'

'You're a bad man, Johnny,' said the hawk-nosed guy, grinning.

'But don't worry,' leered the freckle-faced one (how had she *ever* thought he was good-looking?). 'We won't say a word to . . . anyone.'

Jess pulled her arm free and covered her face. What had she been *thinking* of? This was Shannon's boyfriend. And now, boys being boys, it was going to be all over the school that she'd tried to steal him. Vaguely, she was aware of Johnny getting up from beside her, going over to the others and whispering urgently. When she looked up, they were gone.

'Jess, I'm really sorry. What can I say? They're morons. Total idiots.'

'I have to go,' said Jess, rising to her feet. 'I don't even know what I'm doing here. Sorry.'

Yet again, he grabbed her wrist.

'Johnny, please. I have to go.'

'Just let me explain.'

'There's nothing to explain. You're Shannon's boyfriend and I shouldn't be here with you. Those guys are going to tell everyone what they saw and she'll hate me even more. And you know what? She'll be right to. Now please let me go.'

'I'll let you go if you'll promise to listen.'

'OK,' she said numbly. 'Two minutes.'

He released her, and they sat down.

'Look, what I was saying. I really like you and, as far as I'm concerned, Shannon and I are done. But with her parents breaking up I can't hit her with that right now. It would be like . . . kicking her when she's down.'

'She's going to hear anyway,' said Jess, nodding at the empty doorway.

'They won't say anything. Seriously, I know those guys are total dogs, but they get the situation, and they'll keep their mouths shut.'

She looked at him doubtfully. 'That's not going to stop Shannon hating me. And how many other girls have you put these moves on? How about Paige? Poppy?'

'Seriously, those two aren't even in the picture. And, as for Shannon, it's my fault she acts like that, not yours. First thing she sees this term is me staring after you. So she says, "She's pretty," and I'm like, "Yeah, she really is" – totally falling into the trap – and of course she completely goes off. She's had this horrible drive up from London with her mum, all the stuff about the separation, and all I can say is how great-looking the new girl is.'

'And then, barely two hours later, I go and cover her with food in front of the whole school,' breathed Jess despairingly.

'Well, yeah. That was kind of unfortunate. She was never going to be your best friend after that.'

Jess felt light-headed, as if the floor had suddenly vanished from beneath her feet. She couldn't stay there a moment longer. Grabbing her script, she ran out of the hall into the clean fresh air of the quad.

15

Over the course of the next week, Jess tried to lie low. To attend her classes, work hard and, above all, to learn the part of Titania. The fairy queen had a lot of lines in the play – it was a lead role, after all – and Jess had just a few weeks in which to master them. One of the first people she told about her conversation with Colette Jones was Olly, who hugged her and told her that he wasn't in the least surprised, and offered to rehearse with her any time she wanted. In fact, he said, it would help him as he hoped to be cast in the comedy role of Nick Bottom the weaver.

Soon the *Midsummer Night's Dream* script was torn and dog-eared, with scribbled notes in the margins and Titania's lines highlighted in pink Magic Marker. The words of Shakespeare's play sounded strange in Jess's ears as she read and recited them, but something about their dancing rhythm seemed familiar, as if she'd heard them before, although she was pretty sure that she hadn't.

Jess's room-mates were thrilled that she'd been given such an exciting chance, although they were careful to give the impression they'd known all along that something like this would soon come her way. To help her learn her part, they took it in turns to read through the script with her. Seeing Spike translate Shakespeare into sign language was wonderful. She did it slightly differently every time, her eyes shining with concentration as they darted to and from the script, her arms and hands dancing the lines.

All four of them were involved in the play. Ash would be singing a solo, Spike would be dancing the lead in the ballet numbers and Foxy would be the onstage MC, introducing the production. Only the principal acting roles remained to be announced. Suddenly the end of term seemed to be rushing headlong towards them.

For Jess, working on *A Midsummer Night's Dream* was completely absorbing, and a very good way of not thinking about Johnny. Not thinking about Johnny wasn't easy because she saw him around the place all the time, and everything about him confused her. He'd said he liked her, but what about Shannon? Was Johnny really just keeping his relationship with her going because he didn't want to kick her when she was down? And, if so, did that make him a thoughtful guy, or a creepy and deceitful one? What were the rules on these things? Ash and the others would have known, but Jess couldn't bring herself to tell them for fear of . . . for fear of what, exactly? For fear, perhaps, of hearing something about Johnny that she didn't want to know.

And Shannon? Well, Jess wasn't sure what she felt about Shannon, because for all her beauty and talent she was clearly a very unhappy person. And if she found out that Jess had seen Johnny in secret – and so far Johnny seemed to have persuaded his friends to keep their mouths shut – she'd be an even unhappier person. As for the kiss she and Johnny had shared (and it *had* been shared – she'd wanted it to happen just as much as he had), Jess felt so awful, so anxious and guilty, she couldn't bring herself to think about it. She just wanted to disappear. At least most of her did. At the same time part of her, guilty or not, couldn't quite forget it.

Enough, she told herself, rolling over on to her back on the narrow school bed and holding the script above her. *Learn!* It was Thursday evening, and outside in the trees the pigeons had started the gentle cooing that seemed to go back and forth between them, like a conversation. It was a sound that Jess had come to love, a sound that formed the background of her thoughts at the end of the day.

'We should talk about Saturday,' Foxy announced from the far end of the room.

For a moment, Jess didn't know what the other girl was talking about, and then, in a rush, she remembered. Saturday – the day after tomorrow – was when the four of them were supposed to be going to the film set. To meet Alex Karman and Rachel Manners and perhaps even appear in the film. Thinking about it, Jess felt her heart lurch with excitement and anxiety. It would be an adventure, but it would also be a risk. They'd be breaking school rules in a big way, but they'd also be taking a step into the magic kingdom of film-acting and movie stars. And this, surely, was what it was all about, wasn't it? Placing the *Midsummer Night's Dream* script on top of her locker, Jess turned over to face Foxy and Ash. To her left, she heard the creak of bedsprings as Spike did the same.

'The question is,' said Foxy, 'should we arrive in full make-up, which is actually sort of unprofessional as they'll have someone there to do it? Or should we act like professionals and risk looking like, well . . . schoolgirls?'

The conversation swung back and forth. Out

of the corner of her eye, Jess could see the script sitting there, accusingly, on her locker. Leaving the others to decide the thorny question of make-up or no make-up, she reached for it, and flipped through the pages until she found her final scene with Oberon. Soon she was the fairy queen: powerful, beautiful and in love.

16

Walking into the dining hall next day, Jess felt cautiously optimistic. Overall, the morning had gone well. In ballet class she'd won something close to a compliment from Miss Pearl – 'Better, Jessica,' she'd said as Jess completed a tricky pointe-work routine with a neat double pirouette – and while academic classes hadn't been so great, and French verbs remained pretty much a mystery, singing had gone brilliantly, thanks to Olly, and she'd managed to swing through a solo rendition of 'Lullaby on Broadway' with a relaxed smile on her face and a really not-too-bad American accent. For the first time, she felt that she was keeping pace with the other students. That Colette Jones's belief in her wasn't entirely misplaced, and that she truly deserved to be in the school.

Pointing at the dishes behind the steaming lunch-counter more or less at random, Jess discovered that she had ordered cod fritters and vegetable curry, which seemed as good a choice as any and, adding a glass of water to her tray, she made her way across the hall to the table she usually shared with Ash, Foxy and Spike. She hadn't taken more than two steps when she heard it. A low rhythmic chanting, accompanied by the steady banging of water tumblers on tabletops. Frowning, Jess stopped to listen. Who was it, and what were they chanting?

Then she saw them. It was Shannon, Kelly, Flick and several others at the same table. She could see the rise and fall of their arms as they brought the tumblers banging down. And then, at the self-same moment that she saw the venom in their mascara-ed eyes, she made out the single word they were repeating.

'*Bitch . . . Bitch . . . Bitch . . .*'

The chant was growing louder as, table by table, everyone else fell silent. Jess froze, knowing that the inevitable had happened. Someone had told Shannon about her and Johnny in the boys' dorm block.

For a few seconds, which seemed like forever, she just stood there. A voice inside her was telling her to move, to sit down, but she couldn't. Around her the noise rose and fell.

'*Bitch . . . Bitch . . .*'

And then, the tears starting in her eyes, she was pushing between the tables, making for her usual place. She felt her plate skidding around on her tray, vaguely registered that her tumbler of water had fallen to the floor, splashing her ankles. She scanned the room, desperate now, but could tell that Ash and the others weren't there.

'Jess, over here.'

It was a boy's voice, firm and unflustered. She swung round, and her eyes found Zane's. He was sitting alone, a playscript in front of him, and without a second thought she began to steer herself between the tables towards him.

'Sit down.'

Gratefully, sniffing loudly, she sank into a chair and released her tray on to the table in front of her. The chanting continued, and she could sense people staring at her. She could feel their gaze, at once inquisitive, sympathetic, amused and downright hostile. Biting her lip, trying hard not to cry, she stared at her cod fritters.

'Look at me. I know it's the last thing you feel like right now, but smile.'

She glanced at him warily.

'I mean it, smile. Pretend I've just said something really funny.'

She managed a shaky grin.

'OK, now laugh.'

'Zane, please. I –'

'Do what I say. You want to be an actress, don't you? Well, act! You're sharing a joke with your amazingly funny friend.'

'That would be you, right?' said Jess tremulously.

'Yeah. Right now, I'm probably the funnier of the two of us.'

It wasn't easy, and it wasn't much of a laugh, but she managed it.

'Not bad. Now repeat after me: Shannon. Matthews. Is. *Ugggleeee* –'

Despite herself, Jess sniggered.

'Better. Say it.'

She shook her head. 'Zane, what they're saying is *true*.'

'What, that you're a bitch?

'No, that I –'

'Went mouth to mouth with Johnny Finn? Jess, half the female talent in this school has done that. And, bitch-wise, they've stopped calling you any such thing.'

It was true. The banging and the chanting had stopped, or been swallowed up in the general hubbub of the dining hall.

'What d'you mean – *half the female talent*?'

Zane winced, and ran a hand through his scruffy blond hair. 'Look, Johnny's my best friend, but that boy's a dog. Whatever Shannon might think or say.'

Jess felt sick. Some part of her had believed, truly believed, that she was special to Johnny. And, she couldn't deny it, that had made her feel wonderful and even a little bit beautiful. Now, though, she just felt awful. And stupid.

'Sorry, Jess, but I think you should know the truth. Ever since he first went with Shannon, he's played around. Don't think he can help it, to be honest.'

'Well, if that's how *he* is, no wonder Shannon's like *she* is.'

Zane raised an eyebrow. 'That's pretty nice of you, considering what she and her crew were just shouting.'

Jess shrugged, and picked at her food. 'I'm sorry for her, to be honest.'

Zane smiled. 'I can see why Johnny likes you. You *are* special.'

'What's that supposed to mean?'

'Which is also why Colette asked you to learn Titania in *Dream*. Very smart of her, I'd say.'

'Yeah, well, I'm not actually getting to do it. And how do you know, anyway? The cast's not up on the notice board yet.'

'She told me,' grinned Zane.

'Confides in you, does she?'

'Occasionally, yeah.'

'So who's who in *Dream*, exactly?'

'Well, most importantly, I'm Lysander. A role traditionally played by the best-looking member of the cast.'

Jess smiled. 'No contest there, obviously. So who's Oberon?'

'Your friend and mine, Johnny Finn. Comparatively minor role, of course . . .'

'And Titania?'

'Emilia Bell.'

That made sense. Emilia was smart, popular and a fabulous actress.

'Her understudy's Shannon.' Zane looked her in the eye. 'You should go to the rehearsals. If you don't it'll look as if you're not interested.'

'If I do, it'll look as if I'm stalking Johnny.'

Zane leant forward. 'Forget this thing with Johnny. Go, watch and learn. It means a lot to be singled out by Colette.'

After a pause, Jess nodded. 'OK then, I will. And thank you for rescuing me. Really.'

'My pleasure.'

'Will you do one thing for me? Be nice to Ash?'

Zane spread his hands. 'Hey! I love that girl.'

Jess shook her head. 'You boys, honestly.'

'I know. But what can you do?'

17

'Aaaagh!' groaned Ash. 'Turn that thing off!'

Jess reached sleepily for the alarm clock, stopped it ringing and then leant across and shook Spike.

'Is it seven o'clock already?' murmured Foxy, her voice blurred by her pillow.

As usual it was Ash who climbed out of bed first, pulled on her dressing gown, and staggered out of the door and down the corridor to the washroom.

Ten minutes later, all four of them were washed and dressed in their tracksuits and trainers. Snapping her hair into a ponytail, Jess checked her pockets for phone, comb, cash and make-up. Next to her Spike was doing the same. 'OK, let's do it,' said Foxy, taking a deep breath, and they moved as one for the door.

Outside, the day was fresh and clear. A faint mist hung over the dew-drenched lawns. The pre-breakfast run was a routine that none of them usually bothered with, and the handful of runners already out on the path looked up at them with brief surprise. Just to be on the safe side the four completed two full circuits of the grounds, and then, at the point where they were hidden from the others by the woods, peeled off down the path past the amphitheatre. They were now completely invisible from the school.

Slowing to a walk, they followed Spike. She had scouted the wood out, and found an oak tree with low, easy-to-climb branches from which they could get on to the top of the wall. Foxy jumped to the side of the road first, and then Jess, both of them landing with bent knees to absorb the shock. Ash hesitated, looking nervously down at the six-foot drop.

'Come *on*,' hissed Foxy.

Shutting her eyes, Ash jumped, and Jess pulled her to her feet. A moment later Spike alighted as easily as a dragonfly beside her. This was it. They were committed now, and looked at each other uncertainly.

'Come on,' said Foxy. 'Let's catch that cab.' The road in front of them was a minor one, a back route into Pangbourne, and as they walked in single file round the corner, only a couple of cars passed. A minute later the T-junction came into view.

'It's not there,' groaned Foxy, her pace slowing. 'The stupid taxi's *not there.*'

'And it's gone seven fifteen,' said Ash.

They looked around them, Spike gazing into the trees as if the taxi might be waiting for them on a convenient branch.

'Have you got the number of the firm?' Jess asked Foxy.

Foxy shook her head. 'I left the card on the window sill, in the room.'

'That was smart,' said Ash.

Foxy whirled round, her eyes narrowing, but Jess got there first. 'Chill, guys,' she heard herself saying. 'It could just be late.'

Foxy nodded, her face relaxing. 'Jess is right. Cabs are always late.'

'I'm just worried that a teacher will drive past,' said Ash. 'If that happens, we're dead.'

'We could just say we were going for a walk,' suggested Jess.

Ash looked at her pityingly. 'Yeah, like we're really –'

With a faint rumble, a people carrier lumbered into view. On its roof was an unlit taxi sign. 'Here we go,' said Foxy.

As they scrambled in, the four girls looked at each other warily. The vehicle smelt of stale cigarette smoke and cheap air-freshener. Jess wrinkled her nose; Spike caught her eye and nodded. Buckling her seat belt, Ash stretched her legs out in front of her. 'Sorry I was scratchy back there,' she murmured guiltily. 'It's all a bit early in the morning for me.'

The driver looked over his shoulder. 'So, ladies. Where to?'

It took them just ten minutes to reach Pangbourne Station and buy their tickets, but it was a further twenty before the train arrived. The journey to Richmond seemed to take forever, and involved a change and a quarter of an hour's wait at Reading. As the minutes passed, and the day warmed up, Foxy grew increasingly anxious – a side of her that Jess had never seen before.

'I said we'd be there by eight thirty,' she said, slumping crossly back in her seat. 'At this rate it'll be more like nine thirty.'

Shortly afterwards the refreshment trolley rattled into view. Taking a pound coin from her pocket, Spike pointed at the chocolate bars.

'Tell me what you want, dear?' said the woman, looking doubtfully at Spike's bat-girl haircut.

'She wants a Snickers,' said Jess. 'Please.'

'Foreign, is she?' asked the woman, handing Spike the bar.

'No, she's deaf.'

'Ah,' she smiled. 'They're sometimes a bit simple, aren't they. Let me give you her change.'

Jess glanced at Spike, and could tell from her friend's expression that she'd read the woman's lips.

'*What* did you say?' asked Ash, disbelieving.

But Spike was smiling now. Baring her teeth like a vampire, she began to devour the Snickers bar, wrapper and all.

The woman's eyes widened in horror. She stared for a moment, and then, with an indignant rattle of the trolley, marched on up the aisle. The four of them looked at each other and collapsed, shrieking with laughter, as Spike picked pieces of wrapper out of her teeth.

They got off the train at Richmond at 9.15. The sky was clear, and it looked as if a beautiful day lay ahead. Following the directions to the filming address, they discovered a large house in a Victorian square, with a line of trucks, vans and caravans drawn up on the road outside it. From these, an assortment of cables snaked under a tall ironwork gate.

Hesitantly, Foxy pressed the bell. The gate swung open, and they stepped over the cables into a courtyard paved in old stone. Opposite them was an open front door, into which the cables vanished. Out of this stepped a tough-looking woman carrying a clipboard and a walkie-talkie. To Jess, she looked a bit like the Ibrahims' bull terrier.

18

'We're here for the filming,' said Foxy.

'Names?'

'Eleanor Fox, Verity Nash, Ashanti Taylor and Jessica Bailey.'

The bull terrier checked her list and looked at them suspiciously. 'Wait here, please.'

'Regina *asked* me,' said Foxy, a couple of minutes later. 'She said you must meet Alex and Rachel and be in the picture. You and your friends. We *agreed* it.'

'When was this, exactly?' asked Ash.

'During the school holidays. My parents were having this drinks thing, and Regina was –'

'Trying to be nice to the stage-school daughter? Foxy, get *real* . . .'

Foxy's eyes narrowed in anger, but before she could answer Spike grabbed her left hand and Ash's right, and shook them hard. Then she let go, and her own hands fluttered purposefully. Jess didn't catch all the sign language, but she recognized 'stupid'.

'I guess,' said Ash, closing her eyes. 'Sorry, but I –'

'She's coming back,' hissed Jess.

The bull terrier was accompanied by a young guy in a baseball cap. 'Which one of you's Eleanor?' he asked cheerfully.

Foxy raised a hand and he beckoned her over. The others waited in nervous silence. If they were turned away, thought Jess, it really wouldn't be the end of the world. She knew she was being disloyal, but there was something about this whole idea that had always worried her, and she suspected Ash felt the same way. To come all this way, on the other hand, and not even *see* Alex Karman . . .

A couple of minutes later, Foxy came back. 'OK, basically, Regina forgot to put us down on the list. But she says that, if we want to, we can be in the scene they're shooting today. No pay, but . . .' She grinned. 'We can do it.'

'What about the age thing?' whispered Ash. 'Does she know we're, like, *fourteen*?'

'Not an issue,' said Foxy breezily. 'I said we had the school's permission.'

'Foxy, no!' whispered Ash.

'Look, we're cool, OK? Stop freaking out.'

Ash bit her lip, but said nothing. The others looked at each other, and Jess felt a lurch of excitement.

The baseball-cap guy strolled up to them. 'OK, ladies, assuming you're all on for it, why don't you grab some breakfast and get yourselves to Hair and Make-up. I'm Simon, by the way, Regina's assistant.'

'Mmm, this is totally delicious,' Jess mouthed to Spike a couple of minutes later as they stood on the pavement, devouring buttered rolls filled with bacon and runny fried egg.

'And it's totally going all over your trainers,' murmured Foxy, blowing the steam from a mug of hot tea.

'Whatever,' sighed Jess happily. 'I think I'm going to have another.'

'Me too,' said Ash. 'Once we're in costume we won't be allowed so much as a biscuit. Spike, do you want another?'

Holding her half-eaten bacon roll between her fingertips like a squirrel, Spike shook her head.

'Self-control, you see,' said Foxy. 'Some of you greedy-guts might learn from that.'

'Too late,' said Ash. 'Besides, I'm going to be a singer, not a ballerina.'

'Yeah, a *huge* star,' said Foxy, with a grin. She

tilted her head, so that the light caught her flaming red hair. 'What about you, Jess? What's your dream, exactly?'

'Oh, I'm going to be an actress,' Jess said, although she had never put such a thought into words before, even to herself.

Hair and Make-up took longer than she would have thought possible, but it was a lot of fun. For the hour or so that the four of them were in the trailer, which smelt of foundation and hairspray, Sonia the make-up woman and Darren the hairdresser kept up a non-stop chat about other films they'd worked on, and the stars who had passed through their hands. The four friends listened, enthralled, as the pair agreed that Robert Pattinson was 'adorable', Emma Watson 'a very nice young lady', Zac Efron 'a real sweetheart', and Russell Brand 'a total nightmare'. Johnny Depp had given Sonia a pot of jam from Paris, apparently, and Colin Farrell had asked her out.

'So did you go?' Jess asked her as Sonia dabbed at her cheeks with a damp sponge.

'No, dear. I asked my husband but he thought it wasn't such a good idea. Worse luck!' She and Darren both shrieked with laughter.

'And what about Rachel Manners?' said Ash, her hair now full of shiny clips.

'Oh, she's lovely . . .'

'And Alex Karman?' Ash persisted.

The two adults looked at each other. 'Let's just say –' began Darren.

'No. Let's *not* say,' said Sonia firmly, swivelling Jess in her chair so that she was facing a long mirror. 'Now, dear, what d'you think of that?'

Jess stared. She barely recognized herself. Her freckles had vanished, and her complexion was as pale as ivory. Her eyes, which now looked huge, were outlined in black and smoky-grey, and her lips were a frozen lilac. 'Wow!' she breathed.

Half an hour later the four of them stepped out of the truck, blinking and oddly out of place in the morning sunshine. They looked like night creatures, demons from some dark Victorian fairy tale.

'Does anyone know what this film's actually about?' Ash asked, touching her tongue to her purple-glossed lips. 'Or even what it's called?'

Spike, her eyelids lizard-green above silver-frosted cheekbones, shook her head. 'No idea,' she signed.

'All I know is that we're in some kind of party scene,' said Foxy. 'And right now I think we're supposed to make our way to Wardrobe.'

Following the trail of cables through the front door, they found themselves in a smart front hall. Or at least it had been smart, before the film company had lifted the carpets and removed the paintings from the wall. Technicians and film crew milled around, carrying equipment. At a trestle table covered with papers and folders, a large woman with untidy grey hair was intently watching a series of flickering images on a laptop computer.

'Regina . . .' began Foxy hesitantly.

The director looked up and stared at them. 'Eleanor, I didn't recognize you. You look so . . . grown-up all of a sudden.' Her voice was gravelly, but her eyes were kind. 'These are your friends?'

'Yup. Ash, Jess, Spike.'

'Thank you for letting us be in your film,' said Ash.

Regina gave her a faint smile. 'Trust me, you won't be saying that by the end of the day.' She picked up the phone that was buzzing at her elbow, and her expression darkened. 'Yes? Where? Well, get round there. Do whatever you . . . yeah, exactly.'

Thumbing the disconnect button, she rolled her eyes. 'Actors. My *God* . . . But you girls look fab, so why don't you find Gina and sort yourselves out some costumes.'

Glancing at the others, Spike pointed to a wardrobe sign Blu-tacked to the staircase, and they followed her across the uncarpeted floor, picking their way over the cables. Wardrobe had been set up in what Jess guessed was a children's playroom, as one table held several very expensive-looking computer terminals, televisions and games consoles. *Wow*, Jess thought, thinking of the jumbled front room at home. *Not bad!*

In the middle of the spacious floor were racks of costumes, supervised by a man with a peroxide-blond crew cut. Looking up from a copy of *Heat*, he surveyed them shrewdly. 'Right,' he said, pointing at Spike. 'You first.'

It didn't take long, and when he was done they looked very strange indeed. Spike was wearing a tiny jewelled camisole top over jeans so shredded it was a marvel that they held together, Ash was in a flesh-pink lace-up corset and black ballet skirt, and Foxy in spidery black lace. Jess, meanwhile, had been allotted a short, ruffled dress in grey silk, which she couldn't decide if she loved or hated. She began to rub her eyes, but found her lashes stiff with mascara.

'Hmm,' said Ash, staring at her reflection in a full-length mirror. 'Definitely *weird*.'

'It's like a decadent goth look,' explained the Wardrobe guy. 'The idea is that Rachel, who's a singer, comes back from a world tour to discover Alex partying with all these other chicks.'

'And we're the other chicks,' murmured Foxy, twirling happily.

'You and a few others.'

'So where are all these others?' asked Jess.

'Oh, I don't think the background people are called till midday. Regina doesn't want to pay them to sit around all morning.'

'So when will everything start?' asked Jess, a note of alarm beginning to sound in her head.

'We-e-ell. Depends when Alex gets here really. He's not exactly known for his timekeeping.'

Jess looked at the others, who stared back at her.

'I guess we should get downstairs,' said Foxy. She smiled. 'That dress looks deadly on you, Jess, by the way.'

'Do you think so?' said Jess, pleased.

The four of them had just started down the main staircase when they ran into a dark-haired figure making her way up. Seeing them, she stopped dead. 'Wow! You guys look *amazing*.'

For a moment, they just stared. Even though her face was completely bare of make-up, all of them recognized Rachel Manners.

'Er . . . thanks!' said Jess. 'Have you just

arrived?' *Stupid question*, she told herself. *Of course she has.*

'Yeah, just got in from Los Angeles.' She ran a hand through her smooth black hair. 'What about you guys?'

'Berkshire,' said Ash brightly, and they all laughed.

'Well, you look very decadent for Berkshire,' said Rachel. 'Bet I don't get to wear anything half as fun as that.'

'What's actually the plot of the film?' asked Jess.

'Basically, it's about this couple. Alex is a big rock star and I'm a nobody, but with big ambitions. As my career starts to take off, his starts to nosedive, and he gets into drink, drugs –'

'Goth-girls from Berkshire?' suggested Ash.

'You got it. And now I'd better find somewhere to learn my lines, or I'll be in serious trouble.'

19

An hour crawled past, a bus pulled up in the street outside, and suddenly the house was full of 'background artists'. These were professional extras, hired for non-speaking parts and crowd scenes. There were about thirty of them, mostly in their early and mid-twenties, and when they had been made up, and costumed in twilight shades of grey and black, they looked exotic and a little sinister.

And suddenly there was Alex Karman. Jess didn't notice him at first, but when Ash pinched her and hissed his name she swung round and saw him.

He was coming towards them. At first sight he was as gorgeous as he was in a thousand magazine photos, but as he moved past her, his gaze unfocused, Jess saw that his deep brown eyes were red-rimmed and his chin stubbled. Not in a chilled-out, indie-band sort of way but in a slightly desperate, haven't-been-home sort of way. Jess was seized by a sudden mad impulse to run after him and suggest that she get him a nice cup of tea, but managed to prevent herself.

He stopped in front of Foxy, pointing at her as if to say: *we know each other, don't we?* Jess couldn't hear the conversation which followed, but noted that Foxy kept her cool, looking over his shoulder most of the time, and answering him with a vague, amused smile. The two of them were interrupted by one of the production assistants, who cut in and led Alex away.

'Oh dear,' said Foxy, watching them go. She turned to the others. 'You know what he was doing until five o'clock in the morning today? Playing *World of Warcraft* in his hotel. Apparently his character is called – wait for it – DoomSlayer.'

Ash's face crumpled. 'I totally wish you hadn't told me that.'

'I know, it's kind of sad, isn't it?'

'Wow, you people!' said Jess. 'Why shouldn't he play computer games? I mean, alone in his hotel, with no one to talk to . . .'

The others looked at her. Ash shook her head pityingly. 'Oooh . . . We have a serious case here.'

Foxy nodded. 'Just, what? Thirty seconds? And wham! She totally hearts him.'

'I *don't*,' said Jess crossly. 'I just think he's nice.

And maybe lonely. And why are we here anyway? It was you guys who said he was such a big deal.'

Spike laughed and squeezed her hand. 'Don't worry,' she signed. 'We heart him too!'

At that moment one of the production assistants appeared and announced lunch. 'And please, everyone, *please*, none of it on your costumes!'

After lunch Regina set up the first shot. The idea was that Rachel should walk through the drawing-room door to discover Alex amid the wreckage of a wild party, surrounded by other girls.

It took about thirty minutes to set the scene up, and it was a full hour before Alex appeared, wearing skin-tight jeans, boots, a flowing white silk shirt and eyeliner. He looked, Jess thought, kind of wonderful, and at the same time pretty cheesy. When he walked in, with a cheery 'Hey, y'all!', the room went quiet for a moment. Most of the men tried to play it cool, but the female extras stared openly.

Regina seated Alex in a huge, leather-upholstered armchair, where he sprawled elegantly, propped up with cushions. 'OK, now I need . . . um . . .' She searched the room frowningly, her gaze finally alighting on Jess and the others. 'Yes. Perfect. You four. Over here.'

'Here we go,' whispered Foxy. 'Fame and fortune, everyone.'

They were to arrange themselves, Regina explained, on the armchair. Drape themselves around Alex. Stare adoringly into his eyes.

'Shouldn't be a problem,' murmured Ash. 'Especially for you, Jess.'

Jess stared daggers at her, and Alex laughed. 'Come on, girls,' he grinned. 'Make yourselves comfortable!'

Easier said than done. The leather arms of the chair were worn and shiny, and the four of them kept slipping off. Eventually they found that the best way to do it was to have Foxy and Spike at the back, leaning inwards, for Ash to sit on one arm of the chair, and for Jess to squash into the seat with her legs over Alex's.

'Well, this is cosy!' he said. 'What're your names anyway?'

They told him, but it was clear to Jess that Alex was really only interested in Foxy. The rest of them might just as well not have been there.

'Why don't you two swap places?' he said to Jess, jerking a thumb at Foxy.

Jess's eyes widened, shocked at the brutality of his tone, and she glanced questioningly at Foxy. Her friend just yawned. 'I'm fine up here, thanks,' she said.

'Whatever,' grunted Alex, and closed his eyes.

Jess studied him for a moment, noting the

sulky down-twist to his mouth. *Honestly*, she thought. *He's just like a child who's been told he can't have an ice cream.* Exchanging a glance with Ash, she could tell that the other girl was thinking the same thing.

Jess forced herself to smile. She was going to be an actress, so she might as well start acting. Even if Alex obviously preferred Foxy. Looking around her, she saw that the scene was almost set. The room was an artfully composed wreck, with bottles everywhere, half-eaten plates of food on the floor and paintings hanging askew. Around the room were the other 'guests'. Some were drinking, some were talking or texting, but most were just draped over the expensive furniture, passed out.

Regina clapped her hands. They were doing a run-through, she told them, and explained that when Rachel walked into the room no one was to take the slightest bit of notice of her. They should just carry on with what they were doing and ignore her. And of course, it went without saying, no one should look at the camera.

There were nods of agreement, and one of the production assistants went round the room with a smoke machine, puffing little grey clouds around the guests. The lights were lowered, and ghostly chill-out music played. 'First positions,' called

Regina, crouched in a corner of the room with the cameraman. 'And . . . *Action!*'

There was a short pause, and Rachel stepped into the half-darkened room, looking around her in wide-eyed shock for a moment before starting to pick her way between the dim figures of the guests. Not that Jess saw her doing this. She was too busy staring into Alex Karman's eyes as he started, rather mechanically, to play with her hair. It wasn't a very nice sensation at all; it made her head itch. Nor was it particularly easy to look into his eyes, given that he was turning his head quite hard to the right so that he could look into Foxy's.

'Chris . . .' whispered Rachel.

This was Alex's name in the film and, hearing it, he swung round to meet Rachel's gaze.

'Stacey,' he said flatly. 'You're here.'

'What's . . . going on?' she asked. 'Who are all these . . . *people*?'

His eyes narrowed, and Jess could see him weighing up the situation. 'Just friends,' he said with a shrug. 'Just . . . y'know.' He gave her the ghost of a cocky smile. 'So how've you been? How was the tour?'

'The tour was fine,' she said. 'We can discuss it tomorrow, if you like. Right now I'm going to a hotel.'

'Stacey,' he said imploringly, looking round the

room as if seeing the disorder for the first time. 'Don't be like that. I'll get rid of them. I'll –'

'Goodnight, Chris. I'll see you tomorrow morning.' And with that she turned on her heel and left the room.

'And . . . *Cut!*' Regina stood up. 'OK, people, going for a take. Let's make it *good*. First positions.'

They repeated the scene several times and, as they did so, Jess noticed that Alex was getting more and more tense. She realized, instinctively, it was to do with Foxy. Her coolness, Jess knew, was because she was actually a little afraid of him. But she could also see that Alex read it as lack of interest and, because he was used to people adoring him, it was driving him slightly nuts.

'So d'you wanna act?' he asked her in a break between shots. 'Prop'ly, I mean. Not just as an extra?'

'Not really,' said Foxy vaguely, running her fingers through the red-gold cascade of her hair. 'You need to talk to Jess. She's our actress.'

'I'm tryin' to talk to *you*,' said Alex tetchily. 'What d'you want to do then, if you don't want to act?'

'Oh . . . I'm sure something will come along. Some kind of TV presenter-type thing perhaps.'

'It's not that easy,' he sneered. 'Things don't just . . . "come along".'

'They will for Foxy,' said Jess. 'She has Star Quality.'

'Think so, do you?'

'Don't you?' asked Jess sweetly.

Spike sniggered, and Alex swung round to face her. He was just about to say something – something nasty, Jess guessed – when Regina raised her hand, signalling the next take.

Jess glanced at Ash, who raised her eyebrows. Foxy was right. Alex Karman was not quite as all-round fabulous as they'd imagined.

And things got worse. In the middle of the next take, as Rachel walked towards him, he suddenly stood up.

'Cut,' said Regina. 'Is something the matter, Alex, darling?'

'This just isn't working.'

Regina looked at him for a moment and spoke to her assistant, who told everyone to take five. Jess glanced at her watch. It was almost two thirty.

20

'This cake is divine,' said Ash, a few minutes later. Along with most of the cast, the four of them were sitting in the garden, enjoying the afternoon sun.

'Unlike Alex,' said Foxy, sipping at a Styrofoam cup of tea. 'Boy, what a pain that guy is.'

'You could be a *bit* nicer to him,' murmured Ash, licking cake crumbs from her lips.

'Not gonna happen. He totally creeps me out.'

Suddenly there was shouting from inside the house. '*Why?* Because the way the scene's written, it doesn't bloody *work*, that's *why*!' The voice was Alex Karman's.

A moment later Rachel walked out of the back door, looking pale.

'What's happening?' asked Jess.

'Script issues,' said Rachel dryly.

'What's that mean?'

'It means that Alex wants to cause trouble.'

Spike tilted her head questioningly. There was more shouting from inside the house.

Rachel shrugged. She seemed to have figured out that Spike was deaf. 'Probably feels the camera's not on him enough. Or that the scene makes him look bad in some way.'

'So what happens now?' asked Ash.

'Well, the way it's been before is that he shouts for a bit, and then goes to his trailer and plays computer games until Regina agrees to what he wants.'

'He has a whole trailer to himself?'

'Yup, parked outside on the street. Just for him.'

Ash nodded, impressed.

Jess caught Spike's eye and the two of them grinned. Each knew what the other was thinking: that Ash was wondering how long it would be before she had a trailer of her own, like Alex Karman. Jess also noticed that some of the other 'background artists' didn't look too happy that the four of them were hanging out with a star like Rachel. *Whatever*, she thought. *Let them be jealous.*

'Do you think Regina will agree this time?' she asked Rachel.

'I think she's probably already shot the scene the way she wants it, so yes, I think she will.'

Foxy shook her head. 'And meanwhile the rest of us just have to sit around and wait?'

‘’Fraid so,’ said Rachel. She yawned and stretched. ‘Tell you what, why don’t you guys come to my trailer?’

‘Cool,’ said Foxy. ‘We’d love to.’

Within minutes, the four of them had their feet up in the air-conditioned trailer, sipping ice-cold Cokes from Rachel’s fridge and watching a chat show on her huge TV. Rachel herself was on the phone, drinking iced mineral water from a tall glass.

Jess was so comfortable that she felt herself drifting off. It might have been for a minute, it might have been for quarter of an hour, but when she opened her eyes Rachel was nowhere to be seen, the chat show had finished and a newsreader was talking about a Tube strike the following weekend.

‘What time is it?’ she asked, blinking.

‘Three fifteen,’ signed Spike.

Jess was considering the significance of this when the trailer door opened. It was Rachel, and from the expression on her face it was clear that the news was not good.

‘Alex has gone off in his car, apparently.’

Foxy stood. ‘We should leave you alone,’ she told Rachel. ‘Thank you for the drinks.’

‘No, don’t be silly. Stay. It’s nice to have some company. You guys are a lot closer to my age than most of these film people.’

'What Foxy means,' said Jess, 'is that we kind of *have* to go. Our school doesn't know we're here. And if we're not back for roll-call by six o'clock we are going to be in, like, *major* trouble.'

'Ah,' said Rachel slowly. 'Right. I see. And which school would that be, as a matter of interest?'

'Arcadia.'

She grinned and shook her head. 'I should have guessed. I've worked with quite a few ex-Arcadians, and they're all nutty. Talented, but nutty.' She frowned. 'The thing of it is, you can't really leave now that you're all established in the scene. The continuity wouldn't work. They'd have to shoot all today's scenes from the beginning again, and if that happened Regina would . . .' She winced. 'Trust me, it wouldn't be good.'

'We could probably push it to four o'clock?' said Foxy hesitantly.

Rachel frowned. 'Look, I'll tell you what I'll do. Providing Alex gets back here soon we should finish about five. And then I'll get my driver to run you back to the school. How's that?'

Ash stared at her. 'That would be . . .'

'Totally brilliant!' said Foxy, as Jess and Spike nodded their agreement. 'Thank you *so* much. Wow!'

'Well, that's settled then. I'm just going to have

a word with Regina. Help yourselves to anything you want.'

'Wow, she's super-nice, isn't she?' said Jess when Rachel had gone.

'And he's super-not,' said Foxy. 'If he doesn't get back here soon, we're fried, with or without Rachel's driver.'

As the minutes ticked past, the four girls tried to lose themselves in old episodes of *The Simpsons*, but it was no good. By half past four, a steady sense of dread had lodged itself behind Jess's ribs.

At twenty to five, Spike picked up the control and turned off Rachel's TV. The others looked at her. 'Spike's right,' said Jess, her voice shaky. 'We have to decide what we're going to do.'

'Go and see Regina,' suggested Foxy. 'Explain the situation.'

They trooped downstairs, and eventually found the director talking to the cameraman in the front garden. As Jess approached, the gate swung open. It was Alex Karman.

'Ah, there you are!' said Regina lightly, as if he'd been missing for two minutes rather than two hours.

'I've been by the river,' said Alex. 'Walking. It's so *pretty* down there.'

'Yes, isn't it,' said Regina.

'And I've worked the whole scene out so that it, you know . . . *works*.'

'That's fantastic, darling. Do tell me.'

Jess could tell she was furious, but, oddly, Alex didn't seem to notice. And he got his way because, a few minutes later, Regina announced that they were going to shoot the last scene again, from the beginning.

The four girls looked at each other. 'We're never going to make it back now,' whispered Ash. 'Our only chance was Rachel's driver dropping us off. Now we're stuck here for at least another two hours. I could kill that Alex Karman. Who does he think he is?'

'He thinks he's a movie star,' said Foxy. 'And he's right. He's the reason that people will come and see this film, and that gives him a lot of –'

'Power,' signed Spike grimly.

'Well, I'm totally not going to be like that when I'm famous,' said Ash.

'You totally are,' said Foxy.

Jess stared at them. Didn't they realize the trouble they were in? That *she* was in, especially? Had they forgotten that she was on a term's trial? If this worked out badly – and it looked as if it was going to be working out *really* badly – then her Arcadia career, and all her dreams, were over. All of a sudden she couldn't bear their company for another second. Pushing through a crowd of extras she made her way to the back door and the garden. She had to be alone, if only for a minute or two.

Outside, she sat down on a stone garden seat. The heat had gone out of the day, but the stone was still warm from the afternoon's sunshine. She was furious. Furious with Alex, for turning out to be such a total creep, furious with the others for going along with Foxy's crazy plan, and most of all, furious with herself. As far as Arcadia was concerned, she'd blown it. There was no way they would let her back for a second term now.

Unable to stop herself, too angry and frustrated to think straight, she began to weep. Felt hot tears running down her nose, and saw them fall, as if in slow motion, to the warm paving stones. After a time – a minute, five minutes – she saw a shadow cross the stone seat.

It was Spike. Silently she sat down and put an arm round Jess's shoulders.

'We shouldn't have done this,' muttered Jess, half-turning so that the other girl could read her lips. 'We shouldn't have come here.'

Spike shrugged. 'That is a great dress,' she signed, smoothing the grey silk.

Despite herself, Jess laughed. 'Yeah, we may be

in the worst trouble of our lives, but at least we look fabulous!'

By the time they were inside, Foxy had rung the school. She'd spoken to Wanda Allen who had told her, in a voice that was controlled but clearly very angry indeed, that the four of them should stay where they were, and that someone would come and pick them up.

When they went back on to the set, it was with a feeling of dread. Who would the school send? What would their punishment be? Whatever happened to the others, Jess was sure, her own days at Arcadia were numbered.

'OK, guys.' Regina came bounding up to them. 'Bit of a change to the script. You two' – she pointed at Foxy and Jess – 'now have a couple of lines. Sit down and I'll run them by you.'

It took almost forty minutes to sort out the changes. Learning the lines was the least of it; there were complex changes of lighting and camerawork to be dealt with, and everything to do with filming, as the four of them were discovering, happened in agonizingly slow motion. But, to Jess, the new material definitely improved the scene. And, although it didn't make up for the fact that she was certainly going to be expelled from the only school she'd ever wanted to go to, it was pretty cool to be acting – really acting, with proper words to say – in a proper film. *Thanks, Alex*, she thought. *I knew you were one of the good guys. Sort of.*

Finally they were ready to go. Once again the production assistant hurried round with her smoke machine. The lights went down, the chill-out music played, and the walls of the room seemed to vanish into the haze. 'First positions,' called Regina. 'And . . . *Action!*'

Rachel stepped into the room, looked around her, and made her way slowly towards Alex. Once again, he was staring at Foxy while playing with Jess's hair. Once again, it made her head itch and she longed to have a really good scratch.

'Chris . . .' said Rachel, her voice tight.

'Stacey. You're here.'

'What's going on? Who are all these people?'

'Just . . . y'know, friends. So how've you been? How was the tour?'

'The tour was fine. I'll tell you about it tomorrow. Right now I'm going to a hotel.'

'What's got into her?' drawled Foxy, watching Rachel's retreating figure.

'She needs to, like, get a life,' said Jess.

Ignoring the four girls, concern dawning on his face, Alex got to his feet and ran unsteadily after Rachel.

'What's got into *him*?' asked Foxy.

Jess shrugged. 'He needs to, like, get a life.'

'And . . . *Cut*,' said Regina. 'Good, everyone. Ready to go again, please.'

Jess lost count of how many times they shot the scene. And after the first few times she stopped worrying. About how late they'd be, about what punishment was waiting for them back at the school, about anything. Instead, she concentrated on her part. She only had a few words – fourteen (she counted them), and only seven if you counted the fact that she said pretty much the same thing twice – but there were several seconds when she and Foxy were centre-screen and in close-up, and for those few seconds she realized with a quiet thrill, the two of them were carrying the film. And their tiny scene, in contrast to the drama of Rachel's arrival, was a genuinely funny one. By delivering her lines with a kind of wondering earnestness, and ending each one on a questioning up-note, Jess made it clear that her character was a total airhead. Foxy, meanwhile, sounded so comically zoned-out she could have been on another planet.

Finally, after what seemed like hours, and probably was, Regina pronounced herself satisfied. 'It's a wrap, folks,' her assistant told the actors as the film lights dimmed around them. 'Costumes back to Wardrobe, please.'

For Jess, it was like waking up from a dream, and as she and the others made their way upstairs the full seriousness of their situation washed over her like an icy wave.

'Well, we did look fabulous,' sighed Ash, and Spike and Foxy nodded their agreement. Jess looked sadly at the wispy silk creation she'd spent the day in. It was the most beautiful garment she'd ever worn, and she pressed it to her cheek for a moment before returning it to its hanger.

Five minutes later, faces scrubbed of make-up and shining with cold cream, they were ready to face whoever was waiting for them. At the top of the stairs they held hands. 'Sorry, guys,' whispered Foxy. 'Whatever happens, it was my fault.'

'No,' Jess heard herself answer. 'We all agreed to the risk. It was an adventure.'

Foxy squeezed her hand. 'Well, let's see how the adventure ends.'

Downstairs, all was controlled chaos as technicians hurried from room to room, rolling up cables and packing up lighting and camera equipment. As they neared the front door, Spike stopped dead. There, in front of it, was Regina, deep in conversation with the trim, familiar figure of Colette Jones. The pair were talking animatedly, smiling and nodding like old friends. Both turned at the same time.

'And here they are,' said Regina. 'The Famous Four.'

Colette looked at them thoughtfully. 'So, girls. Are we ready to go?'

They nodded.

It's over, thought Jess blankly. *Everything I've ever dreamt of.* Everything. *And it's no one's fault but my own. I didn't have to come. All that I had to say was that I was going to stay at the school and learn my lines for* Midsummer Night's Dream. *The lines that I'll never, ever speak. How could I have been so totally . . . stupid!*

Wordlessly, they followed Colette out on to the street, and past the film-unit vehicles to a minivan with the school's insignia on the side. For the first twenty minutes no one spoke. Colette drove fast and efficiently, a slight frown on her elegant features, and the four girls sat in silence, sneaking apprehensive glances at each other.

Say something! Jess mouthed to Spike, who forced a smile and rolled her eyes despairingly.

'What you four did today was very, very foolish,' said Colette, checking her wing mirror as the minibus drew into the M4 motorway traffic. 'And what Miss Allen is going to say about it, I don't know. She was very angry indeed when I left, and I doubt her mood's improved greatly since then.'

Jess glanced at Foxy. Her friend's eyes were half closed, and the motorway lighting had turned her features a sickly yellow. Beyond her, Ash stared expressionlessly at the passing traffic.

'What I do know, though, is what Regina Perry told me,' Colette continued. 'Which was that you behaved professionally throughout and, when asked to perform, you rose to the occasion. She played your scene back to me and, setting aside the fact that you didn't actually have permission to be there, I would agree with her.'

Jess risked another look at Spike, but found Colette's steady gaze in the mirror instead.

'Whether, in the eyes of Miss Allen, that will be enough to save you from expulsion, I can't say. I will tell her what I've told you, and it may or it may not influence her decision. Beyond that . . .' She shrugged and shook her head.

'Thank you,' said Jess, and the others murmured their own thanks. Nothing else was said. They arrived back at the the school shortly after midnight.

21

The next morning, after breakfast, the four of them were summoned to Wanda Allen's office. None of them had eaten much – Jess had managed half a bowl of Frosties and a cup of tea – and the occasion was made even more wretched by everyone staring at them. Inevitably, the word had got round, and the whole school knew about the trouble they were in. Glancing about the dining hall, Jess saw the same fearful awe on every face. And the same thought: *Thank God it's not me*. Even in Shannon's superior *Vogue*-model gaze, it seemed to Jess, there was a tiny sliver of sympathy. Not that Shannon was ever going to express it, of course. It was as if the four of them were carrying some terrible, infectious disease. Expulsionitis. Come near us and you'll catch it.

At nine o'clock on the dot, Wanda Allen opened the office door and beckoned them in. Heart pounding, Jess followed the others as they lined up in front of Miss Allen's desk. Not daring to meet Miss Allen's unsmiling gaze, she allowed her eyes to wander around the framed photographs of the famous actors, singers and dancers who had been through the school. One day, had things been otherwise, her photo might have hung on that wall. *Dad*, she thought. *What am I going to tell Dad?* After all that had happened with Mum, she couldn't let him down. But now she had.

'All right, Eleanor, Verity, Jessica, Ashanti, let's get straight to the point. Yesterday, you knowingly broke school rules by leaving the premises without permission, travelling to London, and taking part in a film production not sanctioned by the school. Do any of you deny this?'

None of them spoke. Jess, her eyes lowered, slowly shook her head.

'I'm deeply disappointed by the four of you. We have rules for a reason. And one of those reasons is to protect you . . .'

Miss Allen's voice was quiet but insistent as she explained why the adventure of the day before represented the worst decision of their lives. She had been an actress once, Jess remembered, and knew exactly how to pitch her words to maximum effect. Glancing sideways out of the window, past Foxy's expressionless profile, Jess saw that a fine mist of rain was silvering the front lawn and turning the gravel drive a shining grey. The minibus in which they'd been driven home the night before was still standing there, a silent reminder of their crime.

'So . . . can any one of you give me a good reason why I should not ring your parents right now, and ask them to come and take you home? For good?'

Jess gritted her teeth. Next to her she felt Ash and Foxy as rigid as statues. And then Spike stepped forward. Jess turned, surprised, and out of habit flicked a glance at her hands. But Spike wasn't signing, and Wanda Allen wouldn't have understood her if she was. Spike was going to speak.

Jess watched as anxiety and self-consciousness crossed her friend's face. Opposite them, Wanda Allen sat in wary silence.

'It's OK, Spike,' said Foxy gently, reaching out to her.

But Spike bit her lip and shook her head. 'We're . . . sorry,' she said, the words blurry but unmistakable.

Wanda Allen nodded slowly. 'All right, Verity. I know that wasn't easy.' She looked at them one by one. 'I'll be frank. If you can't think of a reason why I shouldn't expel the four of you right here and now, neither can I. But, on the advice of Miss Jones, I'm not going to do that.'

Jess froze. Beside her, she felt the others do the same.

'Make no mistake about the seriousness of your position. If I hear a whisper of complaint about any one of you, or if your averages drop in any subject, you're out. As it is, I'm writing to all of your parents, and the four of you are grounded. None of you leaves the school grounds again this term. In addition to which, you can forget about taking part in *A Midsummer Night's Dream* next month.' She looked at them one by one. 'Am I understood?'

They nodded, and Jess felt a rush of relief so strong that, for a moment, she thought she was going to faint.

'Very good. Eleanor, Ashanti and Verity, you may go. Jessica, kindly stay here.'

Jess stared in front of her as the others trooped out. Wanda Allen leant forward across her desk.

'All right now, Jessica, listen to me. I understand that, as a recent arrival in the school, you want to make friends and fit in. I know you're worried about your teachers' assessments, and I'm guessing that you might have been rather less keen on yesterday's jaunt than the others. This doesn't excuse you – you could have quite simply said no – but it does go some way towards explaining your behaviour. That said, you are still very much on probation here. You have the support of Miss Jones, but other teachers are not so sure. Your singing needs a lot of work, as does your ballet. Over the next few weeks, you have to convince your teachers, and me, that you deserve your place here. Got it?'

'Got it,' Jessica whispered. Under her T-shirt, she could feel a trickle of sweat running down her back.

'Good. Off you go then. Stay out of trouble. And get those averages up.'

22

As the days passed and became weeks, Jess deliberately cut Johnny out of her life. When they saw each other she blanked him, and in the classes that they shared she made a point of ignoring him. It didn't make her feel any happier, but it was time to accept the truth: that he wasn't hers and probably never would be.

As the final weeks of the summer term approached, a tide of excitement rose about the productions that each year group was presenting. Not even the rain, which now fell day after day from a slate-grey July sky, could dampen the general feeling of anticipation. Students were constantly rushing off to rehearsals and costume fittings, and the thump of feet and the plunking of elderly pianos seemed to issue from every classroom. In Miss Pearl's ballet class, the chorus dancers were practising the pirouettes and skimming leaps that they would be performing in the amphitheatre. Everyone looked bright-eyed and purposeful. Everyone seemed to be in a hurry. Everyone, that is, except Jess, Spike, Ash and Foxy.

Jess was supposed to have been in the back row of the fairy chorus, but now even this tiny part had been taken away from her. Spike, meanwhile, had lost the role of the lead dancer, and had been ordered to teach the part to Kelly. Jess watched the two of them one morning from the corridor outside the classroom where they were working on one of the solo dances. Kelly was good, Jess was forced to admit, but she wasn't half the dancer that Spike was. Where Spike made the steps flow like music, Kelly attacked them like a problem to be overcome.

As someone stepped quietly beside her, Jess looked up. It was Shannon, and she was carrying the slippers she would wear as Titania.

'Nice, aren't they?' said Shannon, turning the slippers so that the light caught the shell-pink satin. 'Like to try them on?'

'Why would I?' Jess replied flatly, forcing herself not to look at them.

'Mmm, you've got a point. Why would you?' She frowned as Kelly once again messed up the step that Spike was patiently demonstrating. 'Oh come *on*, it's just a double pirouette . . .'

'She seems to be finding it kind of difficult,' murmured Jess.

'Yeah, well, maybe she is. And maybe Verity would have done it brilliantly, if she hadn't been quite so *dumb* –'

'*What* did you just call her?'

Shannon winced. 'Sorreee . . . I didn't mean that. Just slipped out. But, seriously, what were you guys *thinking* of, bunking off like that? Surely you were asking to be caught.'

Jess flicked a sideways glance at the other girl. 'We thought it was worth the risk, I guess. To be in the film. And to, you know . . .'

'Hang out with Alex and Rachel?'

'Yeah, all that.'

Shannon nodded. 'And now?'

'Now nothing. Just waiting for the end of term.'

Jess couldn't resist a quick, longing glance at the satin Titania shoes. Shannon caught it, and a smile touched her model-perfect lips. 'In your dreams, Jess Bailey. In your dreams.'

Turning away, ignoring the still-struggling Kelly on the other side of the window, she marched off down the corridor. Watching her go, Jess felt a sharpness behind her eyes. Furious with herself, she turned away, but not before a warm tear had rolled down one cheek. 'No!' she muttered, feeling in the pocket of her tracksuit for a tissue. '*No!*'

'Really not?' said a familiar voice.

She swung round. Olly, a Styrofoam cup in his hand, was watching her with calm, amused eyes.

Jess sniffed and stared back. 'You again! Why do you have to appear every time I'm –'

'In floods of tears? I know, funny, isn't it?'

'I am *not* in floods of tears,' said Jess, smearing a hand across her face. 'I'm fine!'

'Right,' said Olly, glancing into the studio. 'Well, I was just about to leave Spike a cup of tea. So, when I've done that, perhaps you'd like to come to the dining hall and let me buy you one too?'

Jess managed a grin. 'I guess an invitation like that doesn't come along every day.'

By the time they got there she felt better. There was something wise about Olly, she decided. He had a way of letting you know that things were never quite as bad as they seemed to be.

'So,' he said, when they'd bought their teas and were installed on a bench outside. 'Romantically linked with Shannon Matthews's boyfriend, caught breaking school rules, grounded and deprived of a chance to play the lead in an end-of-term show . . . Not bad for your first term!'

'I never meant for any of it to happen, Olly. I just seem to be one of those people, who, I dunno, stuff happens to.'

He smiled. 'I'd say you're definitely one of those people. So what's going right in your life?'

'Not being expelled. When the four of us went to see Miss Allen, I thought it was the end. Really, I thought my time here was totally *finito.* And compared to that . . .' She shrugged. 'I can live with being grounded. And I was never gonna get to do Titania anyway, so . . . yeah.'

And I wish that was true, she thought. Actually, losing Titania – losing the outside chance to play Titania – had left her empty and sad. It was as if part of herself had been cut away. She missed her.

'And Johnny?'

'I'm just trying to move on, you know? I don't want a war with Shannon, and if he's going to stay with her, I guess that counts me out.'

And that wasn't strictly true either. You couldn't just switch off feelings like a light, could you?

'I guess it does.' He turned to look at her. 'They'd never have kicked you out, you know.'

'You don't think so? Just watch. If I don't get my averages up, I'll be –'

'Jess, you're safe. Colette believes in you, for a start.'

'Really? I'm not so sure.'

'Trust me, she does, OK?'

'Well . . . it's nice of you to say so, even if it's

not true.' She stared down at her feet for a moment, then flicked him a sideways glance. 'Olly, can I ask you something? Why were you taking Spike tea? I mean, it's nice of you, but . . .'

He frowned and then, to her astonishment, blushed. 'If you were trying to teach Kelly Wilkinson a dance routine, I'd bring you tea too. In fact I'd give you a medal. That girl is seriously uphill work.'

'I see,' said Jess, gently kicking him in the shins with the toe of her jazz shoe. 'So how long has this been going on then?'

He frowned. The blush hadn't quite faded. 'How long has what been going on?'

'You and Spike.'

'Nothing's going on. We're friends. End of story.'

'I see.' Jess nodded gravely.

How had she not noticed this happening under her nose? And if the two of them hooked up (and they really would look quite spectacular together, she had to admit) did it mean they'd be ever so slightly less friends with her? Even as she dismissed this selfish thought, she felt a quick flush of shame. If anyone deserved a bit of happiness, Spike did. Even Ash and Zane seemed quite loved-up these days. Was it her imagination, or had things started going better between the couple after she'd had that word with Zane in the dining hall?

'Be nice to Spike,' she told Olly. 'She's special, OK?'

23

That Saturday, confined to the school, Jess, Ash and Spike found themselves watching a netball match. It had rained all morning and the court was sodden, but Miss Allen watched all the home games and Ash had suggested that it might do the four of them no harm to be seen there, cheering on the First Eight. Foxy, busy painting her toenails lime-green, had refused point blank ('Why would I? It's all red faces and sweat. And the *clothes*!'), but the rest of them had trudged across the lawn to Far Field, as it was called, by the school's north wall.

By half-time the Arcadia team was three goals down. Emilia Bell tried to rally them but their heads were hanging down and they had a defeated look about them. The opposing team, a posh-looking crew from Pangbourne, clearly put much more time and effort into games than the Arcadia girls, and their shaven-headed male coach towered over Arcadia's tiny, plump Miss Sim, who doubled as the tap-dancing teacher.

'They don't even have a proper AstroTurf pitch!' one of the Pangbourne mothers said as her chihuahua danced at the end of its lead.

'Yeah, well, it's a stage school,' sniggered her husband. 'Why make the place comfortable when they're going to spend their lives on unemployment benefit.'

Both spoke loudly enough for Jess and the others to hear. Emilia Bell, grabbing a sip of water on the sideline, heard them too, and her eyes narrowed as she gathered the Arcadia team into a huddle. When the second half started, the spectators saw straight away that things had changed. The Arcadia girls seemed fired by a new determination, and the Pangbourne team, previously so intimidating, were forced on to the defensive. Within ten minutes Emilia had netted a goal, and Emma Tucker a second.

It looked as if Arcadia was on the point of getting a third, and drawing equal, when it happened. Emilia was running to intercept a pass, and so was the Pangbourne wing defence, a tall girl with long muscled arms. One moment they were both in the air, and then Emilia's legs were flying from under her and the Pangbourne girl was falling too. They landed with a thud, but only one of the two got to her feet. Emilia stayed down. Lying on the wet tarmac in her blue netball skirt, she looked frighteningly still.

Jess and the others stared. No one said anything. Within seconds Miss Sim and the Pangbourne coach were kneeling at the fallen girl's side. Emilia was moving her head now, wincing with pain.

'What's happened?' whispered Ash.

'Ankle,' Spike signed, making a violent twisting gesture with her wrist. The Pangbourne coach was carrying Emilia to the sideline now, with Miss Sim supporting her feet. When they had made Emilia comfortable, Miss Sim took out her phone.

Waiting for the ambulance, Emilia lay on a raincoat, draped with tracksuit tops. It was indeed her ankle, which was either severely sprained or broken. Within minutes, Miss Pearl had arrived with an ice pack. On the netball court a sub took Emilia's place, but Arcadia didn't score, and the game was duly lost. An ambulance arrived on the front drive shortly afterwards, and Emilia was hurried away on a stretcher.

'You know what I'm thinking, don't you?' said Ash, watching her go.

'No,' lied Jess.

Sucking in her cheekbones, Spike opened her eyes until they were almost popping and set her mouth in a Barbie-doll pout.

'Exactly,' said Ash. 'Shannon. If Emilia's out, she's Titania.'

24

By that evening, everyone knew. Emilia Bell had broken her ankle. She'd slipped on the wet tarmac, landed awkwardly, and the Pangbourne girl had fallen on top of her. She was back at Arcadia in time for supper, on crutches and with her leg in a plaster cast.

In the dining hall she tried to put a brave face on things, joking with her friends, but to Jess, watching from the next table, she looked stressed and upset. A rumour went round that she was going to play Titania anyway, crutches, cast and all, but no one really believed it. Titania had to flit and dart and join in the ballet sections. Basically, Emilia was out of the show.

Shannon took her place, and that weekend she and Johnny spent every spare moment rehearsing together. And then, on the Monday morning after Emilia's accident, Colette Jones stopped Jess in the main building, and asked her to run through a scene with Johnny while Shannon was having a costume-fitting.

'It would be really helpful for him to work with someone else' Colette said. 'I'm aware that the two of you have a certain history – oh please, Jess, don't look at me like that, I hear *everything* – but you need to put all that aside.'

Jess said nothing. Not being in the show was one thing, but not being in the show and still having to rehearse with Johnny seemed especially unfair.

'Good. I'll see you both at eleven o'clock in the first-floor drama studio.'

'I've got singing at eleven with Mr Huntley.'

'Not any more. I need you there straight after your dance class.'

Rehearsing with Johnny Finn was somewhere between weird and horrible and heart-thumpingly exciting. Seeing him face to face – and she'd managed to avoid this for weeks now – she felt a blush of shame creep up her body, until her face burned with it. She heard that cruel chanting – '*Bitch . . . Bitch*' – and saw the hurt and fury in Shannon's eyes, and the sniggering pleasure of Kelly, Flick and the rest of them. If she lived to be a hundred, Jess told herself, she'd never forget those few minutes.

'I really like you,' he'd said, when he kissed her in the boys' changing room. 'And as far as I'm concerned, Shannon and I are done.' And she'd believed him. But going by everything she'd seen and heard since, Johnny and Shannon were by no means done, and the excitement that she felt now was not a good thing. Johnny was Shannon's, no matter how he might behave. She remembered Zane's words: *That boy's a dog . . . Ever since he first went with Shannon, he's played around. Don't think he can help it, to be honest.*

'OK, Act two, Scene one, please,' said Colette. 'From "*Ill met by moonlight, proud Titania . . .*"'

Playing around was right, Jess mused bitterly. For Johnny, and boys like him, it was all a game. So why did she still feel as she did when she saw him? That tight, pounding feeling in her chest. As if she couldn't quite breathe properly.

Stop it.

Concentrate.

You're Titania, queen of the fairies.

Magical. Beautiful. Eternal . . .

The lines of the play came easily enough. She'd learnt them well, and they were in her head, ready. But they didn't mean anything. She was too busy closing down her feelings for Johnny. They were just words. Dry as dust. She could hardly get them out. Finishing the speech, she shook her head despairingly.

Colette looked at her, eyes thoughtful. Jess could tell that she wasn't impressed by her performance. And what made it worse was that Johnny was brilliant as Oberon. Wicked, suggestive, flirtatious, clever.

Her eyes still fixed on Jess, Colette asked Johnny to fetch her a glass of water.

'Use it,' she said to Jess, as soon as he'd disappeared. 'Whatever you're feeling right now, *use it*!'

Jess stared at her, not quite understanding.

'In the play, what are things like between Oberon and Titania? What kind of relationship would you say they have?'

Jess frowned. 'Tricky, I'd say. They love each other, but at the same time they're always trying to get one over each other.'

'Exactly. They're competitive. Each of them forever trying to get the upper hand. It's a game that some couples play.'

At that moment Johnny came back into the room, glass in hand. But Jess had taken Colette's point, and this time, when the two of them ran through the scene, she played it differently. She didn't attempt to hide her hurt and jealousy, and when he asked: '. . . *am I not thy lord?*' her response was savage.

'*Then I must be your lady*,' she replied, her voice icy with sarcasm.

From then on, the scene began to work, and the tension began to hum between her and Johnny. And strangely, unbelievably, Jess started to enjoy herself. As Titania, she realized, she could escape from being Jessica. No one could touch her – not Johnny, not Shannon, not anyone – because she wasn't fully there. She was in another place. She was safe and, because she was safe, she could take all the risks she wanted with the character. And that was fun. In fact it was more than fun. It was pretty much the most exciting thing she'd ever done.

They moved through the scene, and Jess felt Johnny respond. Felt him trying to get the upper hand, as Colette put it, just as Oberon tried to get the upper hand over Titania. But he couldn't catch her. This scene was Titania's, and Jess kept tight hold of it.

'*Give me that boy, and I will go with thee*,' Johnny suggested, flirtatiously narrowing his blue eyes at her. The boy was an Indian child, kept by Titania as a kind of pet.

Jess cut him dead with a glance. '*Not for thy fairy kingdom. Fairies, away!*'

With the scene over, Colette looked at them, the faintest of smiles on her face. 'OK,' she murmured. 'Well done, both of you. Johnny, I suggest you thank Jessica for giving up her singing class to rehearse with you.'

He grinned at her, and she looked away, a little uncomfortable to be back in the real world but triumphant at the same time. Would she be able to do it again on the stage, she wondered? To vanish into her role like that? Or was it something that you had to fight for each time?

'Do you want to . . . hang out for a bit?' Johnny whispered as they left the studio.

She looked at him. 'You mean you, me and Shannon?'

'I mean you and me.'

She shook her head. For once, everything seemed crystal clear. 'I don't think so. You're a player, Johnny, and I don't want to be played any more. I don't want to be miserable all the time, I don't want your girlfriend to hate me and I don't want to be called a bitch in front of the whole school. Cos, believe it or not, I don't *enjoy* that, OK?'

He nodded, the blue eyes no longer quite so icy. 'I'm sorry, Jess. I –'

'Were you in the dining hall that day? Did you see them? Did you *hear* them?'

'No, but Zane told me about it. And, like I said, I'm sorry. If those guys had kept their mouths shut, Shannon would never have known anything about us.'

'Johnny, the problem wasn't your friends. The problem is what you, and I, did to Shannon. And it's not going to happen again. From now on, stuff between us stays . . . strictly professional, OK?'

He looked at her uncertainly. 'That's what you want?'

'That's what I want.'

He nodded, and she watched him go.

Weirdly, it felt just fine.

25

'Overall,' said Foxy, propping herself up on one elbow, 'I reckon it was worth it.'

The others stared at her. It was Friday evening, and the last classes of the term had finished. Tomorrow was Parents' Day, with the performances that the whole school had been preparing for so many weeks. Every student in the school – whether junior, intermediate or senior – was involved in one of the three productions. Every student, that is, except for Jess, Ash, Spike and Foxy. The four of them were on their beds in Room 10, watching the rain beating against the windows. The only sound was the faint tick-tick of Spike's earphones. Outside, the school grounds were a dim, sodden grey.

'Look at it this way,' said Foxy. 'We did it. We went, we got there, we were in the film. Everyone knows we did it; no one can take it away from us. They might all say we were stupid but deep down, you can bet, they envy us so much it hurts. Face it, guys, it was cool.'

Ash looked up from *Vibe* magazine. 'And if we'd been expelled? Would that have been cool too?'

'But we *weren't*. And that's the point. And I know we've all lost out when it comes to *Dream*. Ash, her singing; Spike, her dancing; Jess, the chance of a go at Titania –'

'I wasn't even an understudy,' said Jess, wincing as she dabbed hydrogen peroxide on her pointe-shoe blisters. 'It was never going to happen.'

'Well, who knows? There might be someone there tomorrow from the BBC or Sky. And perhaps he would have seen me doing my compère act, at which point he would've fallen crazily in love with me and offered me my own show. So I've missed out too.'

'Your own show,' smiled Ash.

'I'm nearly fifteen. I can't wait forever.'

Spike sneezed. For the last few minutes she'd been lying on her back, squirting little bursts of Dolce & Gabbana scent up in the air, so that it floated down on to her face and shoulders. Blowing her nose with a tissue, she removed her earphones and sat up.

'What are you all talking about?' she signed.

'Foxy said that it was actually quite cool that we got kicked off *Dream*,' said Ash.

'That's *not* what I said. What I said was . . .'

Jess tuned out. These arguments – there had been quite a few of them in recent weeks – tended to go round and round in tight little circles. She blew on her feet. The blisters didn't look too bad. Outside, the rain was overspilling the blocked gutter and cascading noisily on to the path below.

If she had been involved in the Parents' Day performances the next day, the weather might have worried her. As it was, she felt no more than a vague sympathy for those taking part. It was almost certainly not going to be possible to stage *Dream* in the amphitheatre. Instead, with the theatre being used for the seniors' production of *Cabaret*, there was talk of its taking place in one of the rehearsal studios.

Peter Bailey had rung Jess to say that he'd be coming to Parents' Day. She'd warned him that she wasn't in any of the performances, but that hadn't seemed to worry him. She'd asked a little nervously if her mum had been in touch – the thought of her turning up at the school and making some sort of scene made Jess's blood run cold – but her dad had said he hadn't heard from her in months. Which was a relief. Not that Jess didn't want to see her, but not there. Not then.

Did she really have to take her dad to see *A Midsummer Night's Dream*? To watch Shannon play Titania, and Kelly dance Spike's solos? If only the two of them could go straight home, back to doing the stuff they always did. Throwing a Frisbee on Mitcham Common, bowling at Tenpin, watching *The X Factor* with microwaved meals on their laps, laughing at the celebs in *Heat* and *Hello!*

If only it would stop raining.

The dining hall smelt of chicken nuggets and wet hair, and the windows had steamed up. Conversation was louder than usual, with the excited chatter constantly rising to shrieks of laughter. Pre-Parents' Day hysteria, Jess guessed. Well, she didn't feel hysterical. She felt completely blank.

'So what's everyone doing in the holidays?' Ash asked, when they had all sat down with their food. Jess didn't particularly like chicken nuggets and chips, but she'd asked for a large portion out of a mixture of frustration, boredom and sheer greed.

'Home,' signed Spike with a shrug.

'Me too,' said Jess. 'My dad's back from Saudi for the summer break.'

'For the whole of it?' asked Foxy.

'Pretty much. Because he's a teacher out there,

he gets all the school holidays off. The downside is that I don't see him in the term, but . . .' She shrugged. 'It's not a bad deal. What about you, Ash?'

'We're supposed to be going to Cornwall. We stay at this guest house every summer. But we might be going to see my grandparents in Ghana too. Which is kind of fun and kind of weird at the same time. They think my parents spoilt me by sending me to school in England instead of there.'

'What's the difference?' signed Spike.

'Ghanaian schools are stricter. More traditional.'

'Well, you are a princess,' murmured Foxy, who'd been staring out of the window, as if in a trance, at the wet gravel drive.

'Exactly. So it was a bit of a lucky escape. What about you, Foxy? Where are you going?'

'St Tropez. My lot have taken a villa there.'

Jess's eyes widened as she squirted ketchup on to her plate. What would it be like, she wondered, to have parents who 'took a villa'.

'Where is that . . . exactly?' she asked.

'Oh come on, Jess,' grinned Ash. 'Haven't you done your celebrity homework? It's in the south of France.' She peered at Jess. 'Film stars? Million-pound yachts?'

'Oh, right. Yeah. Wow!' Jess turned to Foxy. 'You don't seem exactly thrilled.'

Foxy shrugged. 'It's all, like, deals and meetings and TV people, who are kind of gross. My dad's basically working the whole time. He even takes calls in the pool. God, how I wish you guys were coming. Spiky, can you *really* not make it?'

Spike shook her head. 'Working,' she signed, and Jess remembered that she was helping out at the local dance school in Scotland. Every holiday, Spike had told her, she went home and did classes with the ballet teacher who had done so much to transform her childhood.

And having been friends with Spike for almost three months now, Jess was beginning to have some idea of what it must have been like to grow up deaf in a remote, rural community. The difficulties with reading and writing, the hearing aids that the other kids stared at, the deep loneliness and feeling of apartness.

School had been a mixed experience for Spike. She'd had help in the classroom from a signing expert, who had translated the teachers' words for her, but it had been hard to make friends. And then there had been the speech-therapy sessions, which Spike had found so upsetting that her parents had eventually withdrawn her. One exasperated therapist, forgetting that his patient could lip-read, had described eight-year-old Verity to her father as 'a failure'. But eight-year-old Verity didn't care. Because by then she was taking dance classes in Inverness. Even as a very small child, she had loved to move to music. Somehow, its vibrations pierced her near-silent world.

Ballet became her escape. In the little first-floor studio with its scuffed linoleum floor, no one thought her a freak or a failure, and all that mattered was the dance. It was the one area of life where the young Verity Nash met the world on an equal footing, and she clung to it fiercely.

And before long it was more than that. Aged eleven, she started pointe work, and one day, practising after class, she pulled up into a pirouette, and found herself sailing round four, five, six times – she forgot how many. But she never forgot the feeling. That dreamy, all-the-time-in-the-world sensation of perfect balance. And she never forgot the look on her teacher's face. That quiet smile that said: *Yes. That's it. That's what all these months and years of work have been about.*

It was like joining a secret society, Spike had told Jess. Like going through a door to a place where putting things into words just wasn't important. And, for the first time, she understood the deal that life had offered her. If deafness was her handicap, ballet was her superpower.

Foxy sounded disappointed. 'Really?' she pleaded. 'Can't any of you come to St Tropez?'

Jess and Ash shook their heads regretfully. *The south of France,* Jess thought. *Sea breezes, suntan lotion and expensive perfume.* It might as well have been the moon. Instead she had Mitcham Common, which was nice in its ordinary, everyday sort of way, if perhaps not *quite* as glamorous, and a holiday job in her aunt's pet shop. Still, she'd have her dad to herself. He needed a woman to keep an eye on him. To tell him not to tuck his T-shirts into his trousers, and stuff like that.

There was a long silence.

'Who wants a Haribo?' asked Ash.

The rain stopped in the night, its relentless beat fading to an uneven dripping, and then silence. Lying awake under her duvet, Jess felt a blessed sense of relief. Tiptoeing over to the window, she opened it, displacing a shower of droplets, and let the night air pour in. Looking at her friends in the dimness – Ash with her neat, dark head in the centre of the pillow, Foxy open-mouthed amid a cascade of hair, Spike her usual tangle of limbs and bedsheets – she felt an intense rush of affection. The three of them had accepted her instantly and unconditionally, and she would always love them for that. For making it clear that whatever happened, they were all in it together. And, with that thought, Jess climbed into bed, turned her pillow over to the cool side, and fell instantly and deeply asleep.

26

The day dawned overcast. The lawns were heavy with dew, and the paths dark with the previous night's rain. In the dining hall, wet trainers left a slippery path to the serving counter. Halfway through breakfast Wanda Allen marched in, silencing the room with a couple of loud bangs from a spoon on a table.

'OK, boys and girls,' she announced, her voice carrying to the end of the crowded hall. 'Listen, please! If the weather holds, the afternoon and evening performances of *A Midsummer Night's Dream* will take place at the amphitheatre, as planned. If there's more rain, or the amphitheatre just doesn't dry out, the show will take place in the theatre rehearsal studio in the main building, and we'll need volunteers to set up chairs. Final decision at midday.' She nodded briskly at the silent room. 'All clear? Good. Carry on.'

The four watched her leave, her heels snapping

like drumbeats on the varnished floor. Spike, who hadn't been able to read Miss Allen's lips, raised an eyebrow, and Ash told her what had been said. Spike nodded and shrugged. Whether the play took place inside or outside no longer concerned her or any of them.

'Any ideas as to how we spend our morning?' Jess asked the others.

'Yes,' said Ash. 'Very *slo-o-o-wly* . . .'

Everyone smiled. 'Pack, I guess,' said Foxy. 'So that we can make a fast getaway.'

They had a second cup of tea and then, unable to make breakfast last any longer, trailed back to Room 10. Outside the sun had broken through the clouds, drying the flagstones beneath their feet and lifting the dew from the lawns and flower beds. Jess could smell grass, wet earth and, more faintly, the roses outside the school office, their crimson heads bowed from the weeks of rain.

With all four of them packing, the room was soon in chaos. It took Jess half an hour to get organized. How had she managed to pile up so much stuff? Some of it could stay in the room – tracksuits, leotards, pointe shoes, hairspray, textbooks – but there still seemed to be so much more than she'd arrived with. Eventually she managed to jam everything she needed into her suitcase and, by sitting on it, forced the lock shut.

At the other end of the room Spike was attempting the same task, but so dreamily – sock by sock, hairclip by hairclip – that Jess wondered if she would ever get it done or whether, long after everyone else had gone home, Spike would still be there, picking through her scrunchies and her leg warmers. At that moment a roll of pointe-shoe ribbon fell off Spike's bed, and travelled the length of the room, unspooling as it went. Spike watched it go, her eyes thoughtful.

'Come on,' she signed to Jess. 'Let's go.'

Outside, the sky was a clear blue, and the trees and lawns shimmered in the heat haze. All around the two girls, as they made their way towards the woods, was the scent of the summer morning. Jess knew where Spike was heading, to the chestnut tree, and when they got there she swung herself up after her without hesitation. As they climbed, sun-warmed raindrops fell from the leaves high above the ground. Bracing her feet on the trunk, Jess settled back against a broad, curving tree limb. Below her, perhaps a hundred metres away, she could just see the amphitheatre in its sunny clearing.

Minutes passed, and a dozen or so students appeared with Miss Pearl. They started to run through the dances, working out the spacing on the stage. Snatches of conversation drifted over the still air, and Jess could hear Miss Pearl counting out the timing. '*One*, two-three, four . . . *Two*, two . . . No, Kelly. *Faster* . . . Need to . . . your phrasing . . . getting behind . . .'

Jess didn't like Kelly, but she sympathized. The solo dance was really fast and technically demanding, and Miss Pearl was not about to make it easier now that it was Kelly who was performing it. Leaning back against a chestnut branch, Spike watched the distant figures without expression.

'Pearl's giving Kelly a real going-over,' said Jess.

'I guessed,' Spike signed.

'Are both your parents coming today?'

She nodded, then tilted her head a fraction. 'Why did your mum leave you and your dad?'

Jess frowned. 'I think . . . I think she wanted a more exciting life than feeding the ducks and shopping at Tesco.'

'Bit like you then?'

Jess looked at her, surprised. 'Maybe, yeah. I hadn't thought of her like that.'

'We all want more,' Spike signed. 'That's why we're here.'

'I s'pose it is. Seems such a long time since we were up here at the beginning of term. So much has happened.'

'Johnny?'

'Yeah . . . among other disasters.' She looked away, out across the woods. The dancers had left the amphitheatre now, and the clearing was deserted. 'So how's your love life?'

Spike shrugged.

'Olly?' Jess ventured.

The other girl's hands didn't move, but the ghost of a smile touched her face.

'Come on, Spike, tell.'

'Nothing's happened. Don't even know if he likes me.'

'He likes you,' said Jess.

Spike closed her eyes and, after a moment or two, Jess did the same. The silence was broken by the distant *whirr* of a lawnmower. The sound stopped and started again, hanging on the still morning air.

She had survived her first term; that was the important thing. And perhaps, just perhaps, that whole crazy film adventure had worked in her favour. Before it, there had been a real possibility she wasn't going to make it. That she'd be asked to leave because her grades, overall, weren't good enough. In the last few weeks, though, she'd turned a corner, and it was something to do with what she'd learnt in front of the film cameras. That with a bit of concentration you could leave yourself behind and become someone else.

Someone who could do what she liked, without being blamed or laughed at. And she'd applied this lesson to her classes, so that when she sang or danced she was able to let herself go. To become this other, untouchable Jessica Bailey.

Things started to drift, to fade away. Dimly, she registered the sound of people beginning to arrive. The faint crunch of gravel, the distant closing of car doors. Sunlight began to edge across her face, prickling at her eyelids.

'Spike! Jess!'

The voice was Ash's.

'Er . . . yeah,' Jess shouted vaguely. 'What is it?'

'Come *down*!' Ash called back.

Jess could see her now, on the path, halfway between them and the amphitheatre. Beckoning to Spike, she climbed downwards through the branches and swung herself to the ground.

'I tried to ring you,' said Ash when they reached her. 'Don't either of you ever carry your phones?'

'Sorry,' murmured Jess. 'Switched off. Saving battery.'

Spike reached into her tracksuit pocket, pulled out her phone and switched it on. Glancing at the screen, Jess saw that Spike had several unread texts, and that it was almost eleven o'clock.

'It's Kelly,' said Ash. 'She had a row with Miss Pearl about her *Dream* solo. Said she had to change the steps because they were too fast and Miss Pearl said no way, that's the choreography, and Kelly said right, that's it, I'm not doing it.'

'She said that to Miss Pearl?' breathed Jess.

'Yup. Threw her pointe shoes on the stage and walked off.'

'Wow!'

'Exactly. Wow. You're doing both performances, Spike. You need to go to the big studio now.'

Spike stared at her, as if unsure that she'd read her lips correctly.

'Get out of here,' said Ash. 'La Perla's waiting. *Run!*'

They watched her go. 'I'm glad for her,' said Jess. 'She hated not being in the show.'

'I know,' said Ash. 'And I reckon La Perla hated her not being in it too. She wanted to show off her star pupil. She could have asked Poppy or Paige or Georgie to dance that solo instead of Kelly, but in the end it had to be Spike.'

'I guess it did,' said Jess, yawning as the warm sunshine found her face.

Ash stretched out her arms. 'Mmm . . . I could just lie right down here and go to sleep. But I think we'd better get smartened up. People are beginning to arrive.'

'I s'pose,' said Jess. 'Bet my dad's the last to

turn up. I told him to come in time for the evening performance. I don't want him hanging around here all day, getting into trouble.'

'Mine'll be first,' said Ash. 'Dad hates to be late for anything so he always starts out hours early. Drives my mum mad.'

They made their way back to the room. A farmer's field on the opposite side of the road from the school had been turned into a car park for the day, and small groups of visitors were already making their way up the drive to the main building. The place looked its best, Jess thought. The cloudless blue sky, the dark green of the woods, the faded red-brick towers. Mr Dear, the part-time gardener, was mowing the lawns into neat emerald stripes, and the smell of cut grass and petrol hung on the air. Over the *thrum* of the mower came a faint series of thumps from the amphitheatre as the tent pegs of the backstage marquees were hammered into place.

'Yikes!' said Ash when they got to the room. 'Yellow Peril.'

Yellow Perils were Post-it notes stuck on the doors of students Miss Allen needed to speak to. They didn't always mean trouble, but they usually did. And this one was addressed to all of them except Spike.

Ash thumbed the keys of her phone. 'Hi, Foxy. You've seen the Yellow Peril? OK, see you there in five. Yeah, get it over with.'

When the three of them reached the school office, Miss Allen was occupied with parents. Others milled around, hoping for a word. Eventually her door opened and she came out, smiling her brisk professional smile and shaking hands with a smartly dressed couple.

'Ah, you three,' she said, deftly avoiding the attention of the waiting parents. 'Come in for a moment.'

Glancing at each other, the three girls followed her.

'Right,' she said. 'I assume you know that Verity has replaced Kelly in *A Midsummer Night's Dream*? Well, I've decided that it's not fair to allow her to perform, and not you. So I want you all to report to the amphitheatre immediately. Eleanor, you will go back to acting as compère, for which I'm sure Miss Jones will be grateful, she's got quite enough on her plate as it is, and Ashanti, you will sing during the scene changes as originally planned. Jessica, you will report to Miss Pearl with a view to taking your place in the dancing chorus. Any questions?'

The three of them shook their heads. 'Thank you,' Foxy ventured.

'That's all right, Eleanor. I have the impression that useful lessons have been learnt. Am I right?'

They nodded again, not quite daring to look at each other.

'Good. Off you go. I want you all to do the school proud. As I'm sure you will.'

They waited until they were outside and then, as one, let out a heartfelt '*Ye-e-e-esss!*' Just too late, Jess saw Wanda Allen watching them through the office window. Was it her imagination, or was the woman actually smiling?

27

The rest of the morning was a blur of rehearsals and last-minute costume alterations. Jess didn't have anything terribly difficult to do in the show; she was just in the chorus of the ballet. But the fairy costumes were pretty and she was overjoyed that her dad was actually going to see her on stage, performing.

At one o'clock, she headed for lunch, which had been set up in the quad. There were tables of food and drink in the covered walkway, as well as a couple of dozen rather grungy-looking classroom chairs, but most people seemed to prefer eating and drinking in the sunshine, on the newly mown square of turf in the middle. Scanning the food – basically the usual dining-hall salads, dressed up with plastic bowls of crisps and Twiglets – Jess helped herself to a slice of cheese and a tomato, and stuck a banana into her jeans pocket for good measure. She could have done with more, but the performance started at half past two, and you couldn't really be a fairy on a full stomach.

The drinks table was presided over by Mr Huntley, the singing teacher. There were glasses of chilled sparkling wine, a tea urn, water jugs and family-size bottles of fizzy drinks. Filling a paper cup with lemonade, Jess scanned the guests. Her dad didn't seem to be anywhere in sight, but she spotted Ash and her parents, and zigzagged through the crowd towards them. Ash's father was a tall Ghanaian with the build of a rugby player, and her mum, Freda, was a tiny slip of a woman, almost transparently pale.

'The famous Jessica!' boomed her dad.

'That's me,' agreed Jess, instantly comfortable with this huge, smiling figure. 'Ash tells me you're a dentist?'

'Well, that happens to be true. Have you got any teeth I can take out? I make them into tribal necklaces!'

'Henry . . .' began his wife warningly. She winked at Jess. 'You see what I have to put up with?'

'Oh my God,' hissed Ash. 'There's Johnny Finn. And Shannon. Mum, Dad – I told you about her.'

Jess sneaked a glance. Shannon was wearing a

cornflower-blue halterneck dress that showed off her figure and her honey-blonde hair, and, as it happened, was a pretty good match for Johnny's eyes too.

'Quite a handsome couple,' murmured Freda, and even Jess had to admit they looked good together. Except that they weren't quite together. Because, although Johnny's arm was draped across Shannon's slender back, he seemed to be paying more attention to Flick, who was flirting with him quite openly.

'I think I'll get a gold earring like that boy,' said Ash's father, speaking so loudly that Shannon, Johnny and Flick all turned round and looked at them.

'Glad you like it,' grinned Johnny. 'Hey, Ash, Jess.'

Flick detached herself and walked over. 'Excuse me, Mr and Mrs Taylor, can I ask you something?' she said, addressing Henry and Freda with a sly smile. 'Is Ash really a princess, like she says?'

Ash's father looked at her for a moment. 'My daughter is a princess, by direct descent, of the royal Ashanti line.'

'Wow . . . So do you have, like, a palace and stuff?'

'We do,' said Henry gravely.

Flick nodded, wide-eyed. 'Well, that's . . . that's answered my question. Thank you.'

'Henry, *really*,' said Freda, when Flick was out of earshot.

'It is a palace. It's got off-road parking, a power-shower, Sky TV . . .'

'You see why I love my dad?' said Ash.

Jess smiled, and at that moment Miss Allen's unmistakable voice rose above the hubbub and the chinking of glasses. 'Could I ask that those involved in this afternoon's performance of *A Midsummer Night's Dream* make their way to the amphitheatre as soon as possible, please. Everyone else, please, help yourselves to lunch. There's still an hour to go before curtain-up. Thank you.'

The amphitheatre had been transformed. The stone seats had been swept of leaves, and behind the stage, now covered by a dance-floor, a pair of white marquees had been set up for the performers to change in. Keen to get moving, Jess pulled on her ballet practice clothes. A barre had been set up on the stage, and for the next half an hour Miss Pearl drilled the dancers until the sweat was running down their backs.

Backstage, when they had finished, it was even hotter. On one side, rows of chiffon costumes hung on racks, and on the other a line of trestle tables held mirrors, make-up boxes and cans of hairspray. In the aisle between, more than a dozen girls jostled for space, whispering excitedly, pulling winged green costumes over sweat-damp shoulders and collarbones, knotting pointe-shoe ribbons, and crouching in front of the mirrors with mascara and lipstick. From the boys' marquee, meanwhile, came the sound of raucous laughter.

Why did they always find everything so *funny*? Jess wondered, trying to apply eyeliner as, right next to her, Georgie Maxwell fixed her bun with a choking blast of hairspray.

As soon as she was ready, Jess pushed her way out of the back of the marquee, into the fresh air and the shade of the trees. Nearby, Shannon was pacing backwards and forwards in her midnight-blue costume, flowers plaited in her hair. The two of them were hidden from the auditorium by the stage and the scenery, but Jess could hear a low, excited buzz of conversation as the parents took their places.

'Wow,' said Jess, wriggling her toes in her pointe shoes. 'You look *amazing*. Are you OK?'

'I guess.'

'You'll be wonderful. Just . . . I don't know. Be Titania!'

'Oh, I'm not worried about *that*. It's . . . It's afterwards.'

'Why?' said Jess, mystified. 'What's happening afterwards?'

'My parents, that's what.' She closed her eyes. 'God, why am I telling you this? It's not like we're friends.'

'You don't have to,' said Jess. 'You don't have to tell me anything.'

Shannon opened her eyes and frowned, her gaze distant. 'They fight. I can hear them through the walls. Screaming at each other.' She shook her head again. 'I'm pretty sure they're only staying together because of me.'

Jess stared at her. She had no idea what she ought to say. Or whether she ought to say anything at all. As the two of them stood there in silence, Miss Pearl leant out of the marquee. 'Jessica, please, they've just called beginners for Act One.'

Taking Shannon's hand, Jess gave it a squeeze, and Shannon nodded, her face expressionless.

'You'll be fine,' said Jess, although she wasn't quite sure what she meant.

'*Jessica!*'

'Coming!'

She took her place in the line behind Poppy and, as she did so, heard Foxy's amplified voice welcoming the parents and introducing the play.

'Do my wings look OK?' Jess hissed to Flick, who was standing behind her.

'Well, I doubt they'd get your butt off the ground, let alone the rest of you,' came the whispered answer. 'But –'

'Be *quiet*, girls. Concentrate.'

The music started, and they ran into the sunshine, and on to the stage.

28

Afterwards, Jess could remember very little. There was a moment when they formed a long diagonal, the stage springy beneath their feet, and then, as one, rose on to pointe, their back legs high behind them. For a heartbeat they held the balance, and then, to shivery violins, flitted off in different directions. And then they were still again, panting a little, and Spike was flashing across the stage in front of them, vibrant as a dragonfly.

Jess had very little sense of being part of a story, because every time the dancers went on, the story stopped. It moved forward only when they weren't there. When they were changing costume, or stretching between scenes, or fixing their hair. They could hear the lines being spoken, though, and the applause and laughter of the audience. And Ash singing, her voice bright on the afternoon air.

From backstage you could look through the scenery and see the stage, and watching Shannon, Jess was impressed. The sharp-tongued teenager had vanished, and in her place was the flighty, willowy queen of the fairies. Shannon was good, and she was funny, and when she came on for her bow at the end there were cheers.

Back in the marquee, Miss Pearl and Colette Jones went round congratulating everyone, and saying how well the show had gone. Most of the girls changed quickly and went out to find their parents, but Jess stayed behind to take off her make-up. Shannon didn't seem to be in any hurry to leave either.

'Were your parents out front?' asked Jess, her face a mask of cold cream.

'Yeah, front row.'

'That's nice'

'Maybe. We'll see.'

'So aren't you going to get changed and stuff?'

'I just want to think,' said Shannon.

Jess smiled. 'Well, I thought you were great. Everyone did.'

'Please, Jessica, leave me alone, OK? Like I said earlier, we're not –'

'*OK!* Gone.'

Face still smudgy, Jess made her way back to the dorm block, and a long, cool shower. She was sorry for Shannon, and knew what she was going through after her own parents' last months together, but if she was going to have her head bitten off every time she tried to be friendly, then forget it.

Changed and refreshed, she made her way to the quad, where guests were lining up for cupcakes made by the juniors and tea from a large urn. Spike's parents were there, a burly shaven-headed man in a kilt with military tattoos on his arms, and a slim red-headed woman in jeans and a leather jacket. Both seemed a little overawed by their daughter's talent.

'You were one of the wee fairies, Jess?' asked Spike's dad.

'Not so wee,' said Jess ruefully. 'But, yeah, that was us. Spike, I mean Verity, was great, though, wasn't she?'

'Och, she was awesome!' said her dad as Spike crossed her eyes and stuck her tongue out. 'You all were. We were blown away, weren't we, Janet?'

'That we were,' smiled her mum. 'Are you . . . Is your dad here, Jess?'

'He's coming in time for the evening performance. I should probably go and look for him.' Waving, Jess moved away, but hadn't taken more than a few steps when she came face to face with Olly. She opened her mouth to say hello, but saw that Olly had barely registered her presence. Instead he was staring at someone over her shoulder, and when she turned round she saw Spike gazing straight back at him.

29

Her dad wasn't in the quad, so Jess made her way to the front lawn, where other parents and teachers were gathered. She didn't see him at first, but then there he was, talking to someone's mother. He was wearing a linen suit, rather crumpled after the car journey, and a Panama hat. He looked tanned, and thinner than when she had said goodbye to him at the beginning of term.

'Dad!' she called out, waving, hurrying through the guests. 'Dad, it's me.'

He turned and saw her, and a smile lit up his face.

'You made it! Dad, how *are* you?' She threw her arms round him, felt his answering hug, and stepped back, her arms on his shoulders. 'Gosh, you're so *brown*. Look at you. Wow! It's great that you're here, cos it means we can talk before I have to go and get ready for the show.'

'Jess –'

'I haven't got a lot to do, just dancing,' Jess continued, the words overflowing in her excitement at seeing him again. 'But you'll be able to see my friends. You know, that I've emailed you about. There's Ash, who sings – she's great, you'll see – and Spike, who's like this totally *amazing* dancer, and Foxy, who's . . . In fact come and meet them now.' She tugged at his arm. 'They're all around here somewhere –'

'Jess!'

Something in her father's tone made her pause. 'What is it, Dad?'

'Jess, there's someone I'd like you to meet . . .'

Not quite understanding, Jess looked around her. A dark-haired woman of about her own height met her gaze. She held it and smiled.

'Hello, Jess, I'm Elaine.'

'Er . . . hi!' Was this someone's mum, or what?

'Your father and I met through the university. In Saudi.'

Jess stared at her. 'Hi,' she whispered.

She turned to her dad and saw the hesitation in his eyes. Who *was* this woman? This was supposed to be her day. Their day.

'I should have told you I was bringing Elaine, Jess, I'm sorry.'

'It's . . . It's OK. It's fine. I'm just . . .' She looked

around her. 'I only booked you one ticket for the show.'

Elaine watched her for a moment, glanced at Peter Bailey, and then stepped forward and placed a hand on Jess's arm. 'You know, I'd really like to explore these lovely grounds. I'm sure you and your father have a lot to catch up on. Will you excuse me for a minute or two?'

They watched her go.

'Who *is* she, Dad?'

'She's a colleague. At the university, like I said. We were on the same plane this morning, and I invited her up here.'

Jess narrowed her eyes. 'Why?'

'She's a friend.'

'Just a friend?'

He looked at her patiently. 'Jess, your mother's gone. She's not coming back. I don't want to be by myself forever.'

But you've got me, Jess wanted to shout at him. *You've got* me*! Why can't things go on like before?* 'Suppose I hate her?'

'I don't think you will.'

'Don't be so sure.'

'If you hate her, we'll see. But please, Jess, give her a chance, OK?'

'Jeez, Dad. Give *me* a chance. I don't see you for

three months and then suddenly you pitch up with . . . some *woman*?'

'I'm sorry, Jess. I should have warned you. But . . . I wanted you to meet her. That's all.'

She closed her eyes. 'Look, I just need . . .' She ran a hand through her still-damp hair. 'I'll find you later, OK?'

Peter Bailey nodded. 'I love you, Jess. You know that, don't you?'

She looked at him. 'I'll find you.'

30

Returning to the quad, Jess fed herself a bright blue cupcake, three digestive biscuits and a cup of tea. She loved her dad, but the way he behaved sometimes. This was so totally typical: saying nothing, and then suddenly presenting her with this Elaine person. Today of all days. Honestly, there were times when she understood why her mum had ended up so nuts. Not that she'd ever forgive her for going, but . . .

'Jess?'

It was Shannon. Like Jess, she had taken off her stage make-up, and was still a bit shiny-faced. With her were a tall, fair-haired man and a very slim ash-blonde woman, both designer-dressed. Leaving them with their cups of tea, Shannon walked over.

'How did it go, the fairy dance?'

Jess shrugged, a little warily. 'OK, I think. It felt fine, everyone doing nice clean pirouettes and stuff. La Perla was pleased.'

'No one fell over then?'

'Not even me. How was it for you?'

'Good, I think. Enjoyed it. Yeah.'

'I watched you from backstage. You looked great. Really.'

'Thanks.' Shannon stared at the ground, frowning. 'Listen, I didn't mean to be quite so horrible this afternoon. I know you were trying to help.'

Jess shook her head. 'It's OK. You just didn't look very happy.'

Shannon hooked a blonde tress behind her ear. 'Well, you know how parents can be.'

'I know.'

Shannon nodded. Hesitated. 'Listen, I'm not big on saying sorry but for you, Bailey, a special offer. Sorry, OK?'

Jess smiled faintly. 'For what?'

'Oh . . . That stuff with Johnny. You shouldn't have kissed him, that was *totally* not cool of you, but I know it wasn't all your fault. Everyone thinks I don't know what he gets up to, but I'm not a complete idiot.'

Jess gave her a wary grin. 'OK, well, I guess I'm sorry too. And you're right about Johnny. That totally *wasn't* cool of me.'

'As long as we understand each other, yeah?'

'I think we do.'

'Good.' Shannon pursed her lips. 'Tomorrow, first thing, we're flying to Marbella, in Spain. Where Mum and Dad had their honeymoon.'

'So is everything, like . . . OK?'

'We'll see. They're "giving things another go".' She made quote marks with her fingers. 'You know that routine?'

'No, mine never did that.' She gave Shannon's parents a sideways glance. Her dad had his arm round her mum's waist, and they looked . . . how did they look? Happy? Something like that.

'So we're going,' said Shannon.

'Tomorrow? To Spain?'

'I mean we're going right now. This minute.'

It took Jess several seconds to realize what the other girl was saying. 'But what about . . .'

'Titania? She's yours. Go for it.'

Jess stared at her, open-mouthed. 'Are you sure?' she whispered.

'I had this afternoon, and Mum and Dad were there, but right now I just need to be alone with them. And you know the part, so . . .' She shrugged. 'Have fun trying to get your fat bum into my costume.'

Jess watched her go. And by the time she had thought of a halfway suitable answer Shannon and her parents had vanished.

31

Afternoon had become evening and the light had gone from the sky, but the warmth of the day still lingered. In the backstage marquee, with light bulbs blazing over the mirrors, it was as hot as it had been during the afternoon, and as soon as she had been zipped into Titania's midnight-blue dress – a very close thing, as Shannon had predicted – Jess escaped into the coolness outside.

A great stillness had fallen over the grounds. Around the amphitheatre, the trees glowed a pale lemon-yellow, illuminated by the twin marquees and by the loops of bulbs with which the scenery was hung. To either side of Jess, groups of dancers were stretching against the back of the set, and there was a quiet humming and trilling as the singers warmed up their voices. To calm her nerves, and slow her pounding heart, Jess took herself through her breathing exercises. In her hair she could feel the clips holding the flower garland in place. The twilight smelt of jasmine and Elnett hairspray.

'Ready?' It was Colette Jones, elegant in a floor-length evening dress.

Jess bit her lip and nodded.

'Don't worry. The nerves'll go as soon as you're on stage. Where's Johnny?'

'Still getting ready, I think.'

'Well, enjoy it. It'll never be your first time again.' She was silent for a moment, her gaze distant, as if remembering.

'I will. And, Miss Jones . . .'

She smiled faintly. 'I think Colette, just for tonight, don't you?'

'Colette. Thank you.'

'Just prove me right about you, OK?'

She moved off, speaking briefly to Zane, Olly and the other actors. A few metres away, Miss Pearl was giving last-minute instructions to a huddle of dancers. When she'd finished, Spike walked over to Jess, followed by Foxy and Ash. The four of them linked arms.

'Well, here we are,' said Foxy, her red hair dramatic against her pale skin and chic black dress. 'Fame and fortune, everyone.'

'This feels *so* weird,' said Jess. 'Like a dream.'

'It's real,' said Ash. 'Trust me.'

Colette Jones came over. 'Eleanor, you and I need to get on stage.'

They vanished into the marquee, to be replaced by Miss Pearl. 'Dancers, stand by. Quiet now.'

Spike placed a hand against the back of the set, swung her leg high behind her one last time, and joined the line. Foxy's voice was coming over the loudspeakers now. 'We have just one change to the programme,' she was saying. 'Tonight, the role of Titania will be played by Jessica Bailey.'

Jess tried to imagine her father's face, but failed. A moment later the music started.

The minutes dragged past. She waited, her heart pounding in the warm dusk, half-hearing the other actors' voices, Ash singing, and the applause after Spike's solo. And then Johnny was standing beside her, grinning.

'You all right, Jess?' His eyes were darkened and ivy leaves were twisted into his crow-black hair. He looked wild, and not quite human.

'I think so.'

'Good. Give it everything you've got, yeah?'

She nodded.

'OK,' he winked. 'I'll see you out there. Break a leg, Jess.'

This, she knew, was the traditional actors' greeting before going on stage. To wish someone 'good luck' was thought to bring bad luck.

'Break a leg, Johnny.'

The moment approached. In the marquee, as the fairies took their places behind her, Jess checked her flower headdress in a mirror. A stranger looked back at her. A stranger with slanting eyes and a pale curving mouth. Her cue came, and she stepped out on stage.

'*Ill met by moonlight, proud Titania . . .*'

The voice was Johnny's and there he was, his expression mocking.

Jess opened her mouth, but no words came. In her mind, once again, she was flat on her backside in that ballet class, and the boys were laughing at her through the window. Panic froze her to the spot. If she so much as breathed, she knew, the midnight-blue dress would rip.

And then a feeling of calm rose through her and, with it, a sense of relief so intense that she was almost giddy.

You are a queen, she told herself, gazing at the fairy-lit trees and scenery. *The stage is yours, the night is yours, and you have all the time in the world.*

Glancing at the dancers clustered around her, she saw the challenge in Johnny's eyes, and allowed a faint smile to touch her lips.

'*What, jealous Oberon . . .*' she began, her voice at once silky and blade-sharp. Her smile widened. She was going to enjoy this.

32

Afterwards, when it was all over, she felt exhausted and wide awake at the same time. There had been hugs and congratulations from the other cast-members, and Colette had greeted her with flowers. 'I knew I was right,' she said. 'I usually am.'

Foxy, Ash and Spike waited for her as she got changed, and the four of them left the backstage area together. They found Jess's dad and Elaine among the drifting groups of parents on the lawn, and Jess and her dad hugged, both of them a little self-conscious. 'Why didn't you *tell me*?' he kept asking her. 'Why didn't you *say*?'

'Dad, I promise you, I didn't know until today.'

'You were amazing,' said Elaine quietly. 'Really wonderful.'

Jess turned and, despite the dim glow of the stage lights, saw her properly for the first time. A trim, neatly dressed figure standing watchfully at her father's side. Not too close, but close enough to make it clear that they were together. Jess was about to say something icily polite, something to let the woman know not to take anything for granted, when a question occurred to her. *What is she feeling, right now? What would I feel in her situation?* And, looking closer, she saw the nervousness in Elaine's eyes. *She's afraid*, thought Jess wonderingly. *She's afraid of* me.

'Well . . . thank you,' she said, meeting and holding the other woman's gaze. 'That's really kind. Ash, Spike, Foxy, this is Elaine.' She introduced them, and as she did so, caught her father's grateful glance.

'Mr Bailey, how nice to see you.' It was Wanda Allen, all smiles. 'And you must be Mrs Bailey? No? Oh, well. I'm sure you're as proud as we are of Jessica. One way and another, she and her friends have made sure that we've had a very interesting term. Isn't that right, girls?'

The four of them nodded politely. Olly appeared out of the twilight, and Spike smiled when she saw him. The Taylors approached, with Zane in tow, who was trying his best to charm Ash's mum, and the Fox and Nash parents arrived in a noisy foursome, laughing at something that Foxy's mother had said. A faint breeze crossed the lawn.

I'll remember this moment forever, Jess told herself.

The stage lights went out, and all at once it was hard to recognize anyone. A figure loomed out of the half-dark, and Jess caught the flash of gold at his ear. He was wearing the Radiohead T-shirt and carrying a large rucksack.

'I'll see you then, Jess. Next term, yeah?'

'Yup. Next term.'

There was a moment's silence, and they both laughed.

'Would it get me anywhere if I told you just how good you were tonight?'

'Well,' said Jess, 'you could always try.'

Can't wait to hear more about Jess, Foxy, Spike and Ash? Read on for a sneak peek of their next term at Arcadia . . .

Late-afternoon sunshine lit the school grounds as Jessica Bailey hauled her suitcase across the drive towards the girls' dormitory block. Around her, other students were pulling their luggage from cars, blowing kisses to parents, waving goodbyes.

'Well, that's summer over,' said a voice behind her.

Jess swung round. 'Foxy!' she yelped, dropping her case. The two girls hugged. 'How *are* you? Wow, you look . . .'

And Eleanor Fox, as usual, did look amazing, the red cascade of her hair clashing spectacularly with her pink mohair coat. 'So how was your holiday?' she asked. 'Lots of glam parties, super-fit guys . . .'

'Not too many of either,' admitted Jess. 'Although the boy from my aunt's pet shop did try to snog me when we were cleaning out the hamster cages.'

'Try to?'

'Well, he was nice, but he smelt just a bit too much of gravy-flavoured dog chews.'

'Ew!'

'So what about you, Foxy? How was the south of France?'

'Weird, as usual! Dad on his Blackberry by the pool, turning bright pink; Mum freaking out because they'd asked too many people to stay . . .'

'And you?'

Foxy smiled. 'Under a beach umbrella, covered in factor fifty. The vampire of St Tropez.' She glanced around her. 'It all seems a long way away now.'

'Boys?'

'Well . . . there was this one boy.'

'Go on.'

'He was Moroccan, I think, and he sold caramelized peanuts on the beach. He used to stare at me with these sad golden eyes. We never spoke. It was the perfect relationship.'

'And that was it for the entire summer?'

'Not *quite* . . .'

'Eleanor, Jessica. How nice to have you back!'

Instinctively, the two girls straightened their posture. 'Thank you, Miss Allen,' they replied in unison, as the principal of the Arcadia School of Performing Arts walked past.

'I *never* know what that woman's thinking,' hissed Foxy.

'I think that's what she wants,' said Jess. 'It gives her power over us. But she hasn't totally gone over to the Dark Side.'

'You think not?'

'Well, she could have expelled all four of us last term.'

Foxy nodded as they made their way to their room. Neither of them particularly wanted to revisit that day, the previous June, when they and their two room-mates had bunked off school to appear as walk-ons in a feature film. Everything had gone horribly wrong. Alex Karman, the star they'd risked everything to get close to, had turned out to be an arrogant drama queen, and shooting the scene with him had gone on for so long that they'd had to ring the school and ask to be picked up. Unsurprisingly, Miss Allen had not been amused, and they'd been grounded for the rest of term.

'You're right,' said Foxy. 'I guess that could have turned out worse.'

Jess shuddered. Being expelled from Arcadia would have meant the end of everything. Her dreams of a career on the stage, on TV and maybe even in films. In the end, though, Miss Allen had been merciful, and the cloud had proved to have a silver lining. Grounded, Jess had spent much of the time working on her acting. She'd understudied the lead in the First Year end-of-term play, and a lucky break had seen her step into the shoes of the scarily beautiful Shannon Matthews. For a single, never-to-be-forgotten performance, she'd played the role of Titania, queen of the fairies, in *A Midsummer Night's Dream*.

As if to greet the two friends, the lights flickered on in their dormitory block. Inside, there was a faint chill, and the familiar smell of school. Dragging their cases up the stairs to the first floor, they arrived, panting, at Room 10.

'So, here we are again,' said Jess, throwing open the door.

'Ladies,' said Ash, stepping towards them, arms outstretched. 'Welcome back!'

Ashanti Taylor was still wrapped in her coat and scarf, and, as the three of them hugged, Jess felt a tremor run through her.

'Look,' said Ash, holding out a slim hand. 'I'm shivering. Why can't they turn the central heating on? Seriously, girlfriends, I wasn't brought up to live like this.'

Jess laughed. 'Ash, you are such a princess. It's only September.'

'No sign of Spike?' asked Foxy. Verity Nash, otherwise known as Spike, was the fourth of the room-mates.

'Not yet,' said Ash.

Jess swung her case on to her bed. 'Let's go to the dining hall,' she suggested. 'I'm starving.'

'Already?' Foxy raised an elegantly arched eyebrow. 'Jess, we've only been back here five minutes.'

'That's quite long enough,' said Jess firmly.

Five minutes later, they were sitting with steaming cups of tea in front of them. Other Arcadians drifted into the dining hall in small, chattering groups, looking around as they entered, waving, hugging, and searching each other's faces for signs of change.

The hubbub grew. Further up the table, a long-established trio took their places: Shannon Matthews and her side-kicks Kelly Wilkinson and Flick Healey. As usual, all three were dressed to impress in designer-branded hoodies and T-shirts. For much of the previous term Shannon and Jess had got on so badly they'd barely been able to speak to each other, and it hadn't helped that Shannon had suspected Jess of trying to steal her boyfriend.

Shannon had been wrong; Jess hadn't tried to do anything of the sort. But Johnny Finn was very good-looking, and he had seemed to like her a lot, and somehow – she really, *really* hadn't planned this – they'd ended up kissing in the boys' locker room, and for a split second everything had been wonderful. But only for a split second, because they'd been seen, and shortly afterwards – Jess still froze with horror remembering the scene – she had walked into the dining hall to be met with a chorus of '*Bitch, bitch, bitch!*' from Shannon and her friends. That had been bad enough, but what had been worse was the realization that, in the end, she'd never really meant that much to Johnny. All that attention he'd paid her – all those meaningful looks, all those text messages – had been just been part of his game. He was a player, and she'd been played.

Well, it wasn't going to happen again, and she and Shannon were now officially quits. They weren't friends exactly, but they had a wary respect for each other, especially since Jess had taken over Shannon's role in the end-of-term play in July. Now, the summer was over and the autumn term was beginning. From today, they were all Second Years. A chance to start again, surely?